CAMOUFLAGE

CAMOUFLAGE

A Nameless Detective Novel

Bill Pronzini

A Tom Doherty Associates Book
New York

CAMOUFLAGE: A NAMELESS DETECTIVE NOVEL

Copyright © 2011 by the Pronzini-Muller Family Trust

A Forge Book
Published by Tom Doherty Associates, LLC
175 Fifth Avenue
New York, NY 10010

www.tor-forge.com

Forge® is a registered trademark of Tom Doherty Associates, LLC.

ISBN 978-0-7653-2564-8

First Edition: June 2011

Printed in the United States of America

0 9 8 7 6 5 4 3 2 1

For Dominick Abel

ACKNOWLEDGMENTS

My thanks to Mike White, for his invaluable help with certain aspects of police procedure and criminal law; and to Kit and Arthur Knight, for supplying the impetus for one of the storylines.

CAMOUFLAGE

1

I said, "You want us to do *what?*"

David Virden showed me his teeth in a lopsided smile. "Find one of my ex-wives," he said again. "The first one."

"Divorced eight years, you said."

"That's right."

"And you want her located for what reason again?"

"The same reason I had to track down the other two. So I can have the marriage annulled."

Virden looked, sounded, and acted normal enough. Executive with a manufacturing firm in the South Bay; his business card confirmed it. Forty or so, fair-haired, gray-eyed, handsome in a sleek, metrosexual way. Sitting comfortably in one of the clients' chairs across my desk, legs crossed and one foot jiggling a little so that his expensive polished loafer threw off little glints of light from the overhead fluorescents. But if there's one absolute truism in the detective business, it's that people's exteriors don't always reflect their interiors. Some of the most attractive ones are like buildings full of dark rooms and the kinds of things that hide in them.

"I haven't seen her since the divorce," he said, "and nobody else seems to have seen her in about seven years. Of course she could be dead by now. If that's the case, there won't be any problem."

"Oh, there won't."

"No. Anyhow, we didn't have any trouble finding the other two. They were both pretty cooperative."

"In giving you annulments."

"That's right. I need the third before I can go ahead. Or proof that she's no longer aboveground."

"Go ahead with what?"

"Marrying my fiancée, Judith LoPresti. My fourth and I hope last wife."

I'd gotten it by this time. A little slow on the uptake these days, but prospective clients who walk in off the street and smack you with a job request you've never encountered before are relatively rare. At least Virden wasn't a head case, the kind with no method to their apparent madness.

I said, "Are you Catholic, Mr. Virden?"

"No. Well, not yet."

"But Judith is."

"Devout. Mass every Sunday and the Pope can do no wrong."

"And she won't marry you unless you convert, is that it?"

"That's it. Convert and then have a Church-sanctioned wedding. Only I can't convert without the annulments from my ex-wives because the Catholic Church doesn't recognize civil divorce laws."

"Uh-huh."

"You know about that, right? I mean, your name . . . I figure you must be Catholic. Most Italians are."

"Born and baptized," I said. I didn't add that I was lapsed, for reasons of my own that were none of his business. I happen to believe that religion, like sex between consenting adults, ought to be—and too often isn't these days—strictly a private matter. I also believe in separation of church and state, the Golden Rule, the true definition of family values, that anybody ought to be able to get married regardless of gender, that no one has the right to distort the truth for any reason, and that people ought to quit trying to shove their beliefs and opinions down the throats of other people. Just another crazy old radical thinker, that's me.

"I've never been religious myself," Virden said, as if he was proud of the fact, "but I'd do anything for Judith. She's a real prize." He showed me his lopsided smile again and added a wink to it. "Her father happens to be loaded. I'll be set for life once we're married."

Nice guy, Virden. Full of compassion and the milk of human kindness. I wondered if he was as up-front about his motives with his devout intended. If not, I hoped for her sake that she knew what kind of man she was taking into her faith and her bed.

He said, "Here's the stuff from the Church," and passed a small manila envelope across the desk.

Inside, paper-clipped together, were a two-page letter from the Judicial Vicar of the Diocese of San Jose addressed to Roxanne L. McManus, at an address in Blodgett, California; a Church brochure; a form to be filled out by Ms. McManus and returned to the Diocese; and an SASE. The letter stated that David Paul Virden had petitioned the Diocesan Tribunal to execute a Decree of Nullity, an official document declaring that his marriage to Ms. McManus did not create a permanent sacramental bond and therefore was not an obstacle to future marriage in the Church. There was a list of twelve points informing Ms. McManus of her rights in the matter, among them the right to appoint a Procurator-Advocate and the right to review copies of the ACTA, the First Instance decision, and the Second Instance decision in the office of the local Tribunal. The brochure, which I skimmed through, provided a lengthy overview of the annulment process.

I returned the material to the envelope. When I started to slide it back to Virden, he said, "No, you keep it. Give it to Roxanne when you find her."

"Why not just deliver it yourself?"

"I don't like dealing directly with my ex-wives. You know how it is."

No, I didn't. But I said, "Well, we can make the delivery if she's living in Northern California, but it'll cost you extra."

"I don't care about that. I'd just have to hire somebody else to do it."

Right—with Judith LoPresti's money, no doubt. Not that it was any of my business who paid his bills. "Is McManus your ex-wife's maiden name?"

"Yes. She took it back after the divorce."

"What does the middle initial stand for?"

"Lorraine."

"Roxanne Lorraine McManus." I made a note on the pad I use for client interviews. "You said the last time you saw her was eight years ago?"

"That's right."

"Where?"

"In San Jose, right after the divorce."

"The Diocese letter is addressed to her in Blodgett."

"Her hometown. She moved back there."

"But she's not there now."

"No. I checked and my lawyer checked. She moved away again about seven years ago and nobody's heard from her since."

"Then where did the Diocese get the address?"

"It's her aunt Alma's. I gave it to them—they had to have one for the form."

"But the aunt doesn't have any idea where Roxanne is?"

"No idea. Complete silence since she sold her pet shop and left Blodgett again."

"Does the aunt know why she moved?"

"Told Alma she was going into business with a friend."

"Friend's name?"

"Didn't say, or if she did, Alma forgot it. Somebody she'd just met."

"Male or female?"

"Couldn't remember that, either. Alma's memory's not what it used to be." Virden chuckled wryly to himself. "But she's still a crusty old girl, cusses like a teenager. She had a few choice words for Roxie."

"Why?"

"Pissed because of all the years of silence. Thought Roxie cared more than to blow her off that way."

"Could she remember what kind of business deal it was?"

"No. But it probably had something to do with animals. Roxie owned the pet shop when I met her." Virden cast his eyes upward. "The Warm and Fuzzy Shop, she called it. Terminal goddamn cute."

"Where is Blodgett exactly? I've never heard of it."

"No reason you should have. It's a nowhere little town up near the Oregon border."

"Is that where you were living while you were married to her?"

"God, no," Virden said. "It's where she lived when we met. I was a salesman working the Highway Five corridor in those days, on the road most of the time. She was eating alone in a restaurant I stopped at one night, we struck up a conversation, hit it off, and the next thing I knew we were married. But there was no way I was going to live in a crap-hole like Blodgett. Roxie leased her cute little shop—she wouldn't sell it back then—and I moved her into my apartment in San Jose."

"How long did the marriage last?"

"Two years. Then I met Elaine, my second wife, and that was the end of Roxie."

The end of Roxie. Some turn of phrase.

"She have any other living relatives?" I asked.

"No. Both parents were dead before we were married, no brothers or sisters."

"What else can you tell me about her? Hobbies, special interests?"

"Animals, like I said. Always yapping at me about getting a dog or a cat or some damn thing. I didn't want any part of that, so she started volunteering at one of the animal shelters. Spent more time there than she did at home with me."

I didn't blame her.

"Any other interests?"

"None that'll help you find her." Virden punctuated the sentence with a leer.

"Would you happen to have a photograph of her?"

"Sure. I figured you might need one." He produced it from the inside pocket of his suit coat. "It's more than eight years old," he said as he handed it over. "I haven't changed much since, but she might've. You know how it is with women as they get older."

Keep it up, Virden, I thought. One or two more glimpses into what goes on inside that head of yours and I'll toss you right out of here. I don't have to like the agency's clients, but on the other hand, we don't need business badly enough so I have to put up with greedy self-centered sexists who insist on red-flagging their shortcomings.

I looked at the photograph. Five-by-seven color snapshot of Virden and a slender brunette taken on a beach somewhere, him in swim trunks and her in a two-piece suit. She had nice features—prominent cheekbones, luminous brown eyes, a generous smiling mouth. The swimsuit accentuated her other physical assets, no doubt the primary ones that had attracted Virden.

"How old was she when this was taken?"

"Let's see. Thirty-one, thirty-two . . . yeah, thirty-two."

"Do you remember her birth date?"

"Birth date." His face screwed up in thought, smoothed out again. "I'm not very good with dates."

"The month, at least."

"June? No, July. That's right; I remember now because it was a few days after the Fourth. Sixth, seventh, eighth, one of those."

I asked him a few more questions, and he managed not to annoy me with his answers. So then I told him how much the investigation would cost, resisting an impulse to juice the charges a little. He didn't bat an eye. Hell, why should he? It was small change compared to what he expected to be privy to once he joined the LoPresti family.

He signed the standard agency contract, wrote out a check for the retainer. "So," he said then, "how long do you think it'll take to find her?"

Roxanne Lorraine McManus. Not a common name, and he'd provided a reasonable amount of personal information. "I can't give you an exact time line, but it shouldn't take too long. This is Friday . . . possibly Monday."

"The quicker the better. For Judith's sake."

"Yeah," I said.

"Alive or dead, doesn't matter which."

No, not to him it didn't. As far as David Virden was concerned, Roxanne Lorraine McManus had ceased to exist the day he'd divorced her eight years ago.

After Virden left, I took my notes and the photograph into Tamara's office. Skip-traces and missing-person cases are her meat. I've learned some computer skills from her and from Kerry, and Jake Runyon is proficient enough when the need arises, but she's the resident expert. If there's any information on any subject or person living or deceased available in cyberspace, she can find it as quickly as any professional hacker working today.

She was busy, as always, but she didn't seem to mind the interruption or being handed additional work. There were a number of different Tamaras living inside her slightly plump young body; there were Grumpy Tamara, Professional Tamara, Tough Tamara, Streetwise Tamara, Philosophical Tamara, Playful Tamara, Sex-Starved Tamara, and a handful of others. But what we'd had for the past ten days or so was a brand-new member of the team: Unflappable Tamara. Or maybe Seriously Adult Tamara. Not exactly serene or cheerful, but exhibiting signs of both, and neither bothered nor shaken by anyone or anything. I liked most of the other personas, but I was developing a particular fondness for this one. No surprises, no put-ons or detailed commentaries on her sex life or lack thereof, and no need for me to shift into one of my own multiple personalities—boss, mentor, father confessor, pacifier—in dealing with her.

The reason for the appearance of this welcome new Tamara had to do with her involvement, both personally and professionally, with a con man calling himself Lucas Zeller. The secretive professional part had been a mistake, one that had nearly cost her her life, and the experience seemed to have had a profound effect on her. She was smart as a whip, but in the six years I'd known and worked with her she'd been unpredictable, not completely grounded, and just a little immature. I had the feeling that none of those applied any longer, that now, at age twenty-seven, she'd learned the lessons that come with full maturity. Seriously Adult Tamara.

She glanced at the photo, read through my notes. "Weird," she said. "Bet you never had a case like this before."

"Not even close. At first I thought I'd caught another cutey." Cutie

"Cutey?"

"The oddball cases I seem to get stuck with. Pretty straight-forward, once Virden explained his motives."

"Uh-huh. I didn't know the Catholic Church could annul marriages that'd already ended in divorce."

"It's not common knowledge outside the faith."

"Three exes and now the dude's looking to marry number four. This one must have money."

"Good guess."

"Greed beats love every time for some guys."

"He was up-front about it; I'll give him that," I said. "I wouldn't've taken him on if it wasn't a simple trace job."

"Simple as long as his checks don't bounce."

"I'll run his retainer check down to the bank on my lunch break."

"Low-priority case, right?"

"Right. Fit it in when you can."

She gave me a patient little smile, my cue to go away and let her get back to work. I liked that, too. It was a much more pleasant cue than some of those her other personalities indulged in.

Jake Runyon rolled into the agency a little past four thirty, just as I was about to leave for the day. I had my overcoat and hat and muffler on; the weather lately had been fog ridden and blustery, the kind—even though it was only April—that had inspired Mark Twain to write that the coldest winter he'd ever spent was a summer in San Francisco. Runyon, on the other hand, was coatless in a rumpled suit and tie. He seemed impervious to weather conditions of any kind, maybe because he was a native of Seattle. The fact that he was twenty years younger than me might also have had something to do with it; I hadn't been nearly so aware of weather extremes when I was his age.

He'd been out on a hunt for a witness to a near-fatal hit-and-run auto accident. The agency doesn't usually handle personal injury cases, but the injured party involved in this one was a local politician whose attorney knew a criminal lawyer I'd done some work for in the past. So we'd taken it on as a favor. Quid pro quo is a necessity in any successful detective business.

"Find the witness yet?" I asked Runyon.

"Name and address, but he's out of town for the weekend. Back on Monday—I'll brace him then. Anything new for me?"

"Nope. One new client today, but it's a minor trace job and Tamara and I are handling it."

He ran a hand over his slablike face. Something on his mind; I could see it in his eyes. "You in a hurry to get home?"

"Not really. Why?"

"I can use your input on a problem."

"Business?"

"Personal."

That was a surprise. Runyon was usually reticent when it came to his personal life; he'd offer up snippets now and then if you asked him a direct question, but he seldom volunteered any information.

"Sure thing," I said. "How about we go across the square? I can use a beer."

"I'll buy," he said.

2

The agency's offices are in an old, salmon-colored building on South Park, a chunk of Bohemian-era San Francisco—private residences, cafés, small businesses, a little park and playground—sandwiched among a lot of high-rise buildings between Second and Third, Brannan and Bryant. It was a prime business location, close to downtown and the Bay Bridge; we'd managed to get a long-term lease shortly after the dot-com industry collapse a few years ago, when office space all over the city was going begging. Lucky timing, because the industry had bounced back and now the area surrounding South Park was thick with high-tech companies paying rents five and six times higher than ours.

The South Park Café, on the opposite side of the square, was already starting to fill up with the Friday evening happy hour crowd when Runyon and I walked in. We managed to claim the last available table just ahead of a young couple who glared at us as if we'd robbed them of something valuable. Funny thing was, it was the same table we'd sat at a couple of weeks ago, at a quieter time of day, for the same reason we were here now—to talk over a personal matter.

Only then it had been my personal matter, a nasty bit of business involving my adopted daughter, Emily, that still raised my blood pressure whenever I thought about it. I'd asked Jake to join me in doing something that was borderline illegal, and despite the professional risk he'd agreed without hesitation. I owed him any kind of favor in return.

Runyon had also noticed the coincidence. He said as we waited for service, "Nothing like the last time we were here. Except that it's about a kid in trouble . . . maybe."

"You're not sure?"

"Not a hundred percent. I could use your input."

"Glad to help if I can, you know that. Who's the kid?"

"Bryn's son, Bobby."

Bryn was a woman he'd met not long ago, the first relationship he'd had since the death of his second wife, Colleen, in Seattle. Colleen had wasted away slowly from ovarian cancer, which left him devastated. He'd moved down here to be close to his estranged gay son from his first marriage, but they still hadn't reconciled. Jake's life had narrowed down to his work—he was a hell of a good investigator—and for the first year and a half he'd worked for the agency he'd been a tightly closed-off loner. Bryn Darby had brought him out of that hard depressive shell, started him living again for something more than his job. She was a commercial artist, divorced, with the one young son and a home in the Sunset District; that was all I knew about her, aside from one reference to a "physical problem" that he wouldn't elaborate on.

"What's the trouble with Bobby?" I asked.

This wasn't easy for Runyon. He sat tight-mouthed for a few seconds, scraping fingernails along his hammerhead jaw, before he answered. "Bryn thinks he's being abused. Physically."

"Christ. By whom?"

"His father. Robert Darby. West Portal lawyer, used his position to convince a judge to grant him primary custody."

"But you're not sure about the abuse?"

"Bryn is. Bobby showed up at school with a fractured arm, claimed it happened in a fall. The doctor who set it found bruises on the kid's back and arms. Bobby said he got them playing football with a couple of schoolmates."

"Any other physical evidence?"

"No. But Bryn says there've been personality changes consistent with abuse—withdrawal, that kind of thing."

"Has she confronted her ex?"

"Roundabout. He denies it, naturally."

"Taken her suspicions to Bobby's school counselor or Social Services?"

"Not enough proof without his cooperation."

"Any chance she could get the boy to a child psychologist, draw it out of him that way?"

Runyon shook his head. "She's afraid to do anything that might provoke Darby into legally shoving her all the way out of the kid's life."

"He sounds like a bastard."

"First-class."

"Have you met him?"

"Once. I went to his office a couple of days ago."

I didn't say anything.

Runyon said, "Yeah, I know. But I had to do it."

"Tell Bryn you were going to see him?"

"No. I didn't want to upset her. Or get her hopes up."

"How'd you approach him?"

"Calm and polite, as a concerned friend."

"Tell him you're a detective?"

"No way around it. Friend wasn't enough for him—he demanded to know who I was and I didn't want to start off by lying to him."

"Bet I can guess his reaction."

"Yeah. He went all hard-ass lawyer, warned me to keep my nose out of his private life, and threw me out."

"What was your take? Think Bryn's right about him?"

"Capable of child abuse—capable of just about anything. Acted outraged and protective of Bobby, called Bryn a paranoid hysteric, but the guilty ones take that line same as the innocent."

"Every time."

"That's where it stands now," Runyon said. "Nowhere."

"And you're wondering what I'd do if I were in your shoes."

"Like I said, I can use your input. You've had experience with kids—Emily's not much older than Bobby."

"Well, the smart answer is drop it, don't get any more involved."

"That's what I keep telling myself. But I can't just walk away. Would you be able to?"

"Probably not."

"So?"

"So you've got to be pretty careful, Jake. Any kind of strong-arm stuff is out. So is confronting Darby straight on."

"I know it. He'd sue me for harassment in a New York minute."

"You run a background check on him?"

"First thing. Nothing there. His record's clean except for one speeding ticket and an unprofessional ethics charge that got him a warning from the ABA five years ago."

A waitress finally showed up to take our order for a couple of Anchor Steam drafts. The interruption gave me time to weigh Runyon's problem. When we were alone again, I said, "You've met the boy, right? Spend much time with him?"

"Not much, no. Bryn only gets him two weekends a month."

"The next is when?"

"This weekend. She picked him up at school today."

"Is he easy to talk to, get along with?"

"Shy. Doesn't say much."

"Would Bryn let you take him somewhere without her?"

". . . She might. But if he won't tell his mother he's being abused, he's not going to open up to a stranger."

"His mother's not a detective. You've interrogated kids before, same as I have. There're ways to do it without making it seem like an interrogation."

Runyon thought that over. "Maybe," he said.

"Worth a shot," I said. "I don't see anything else you can do without risking a lawsuit and jeopardizing your license. Except be there for Bryn and the boy."

"That's a given. Thanks."

"*Por nada*. Keep me posted."

He said he would. The beers arrived then and we shifted the conversation to agency business while we drank them.

Emily was alone in the Diamond Heights condo when I walked in, working on dinner in the kitchen. No real surprise there; she often did the cooking when Kerry had to work late at Bates and Carpenter and it was one of my days at the agency. Emily was thirteen going on thirty, one of those rare kids who were not only intelligent but also good at anything that interested them, from school subjects to the environment to music to Home Ec.

What surprised me a little, and pleased and relieved me, was that she was singing while she cooked.

The unpleasant events of a couple of weeks ago, which she'd been innocently involved in and that Runyon and I had dealt with, had had a rough effect on her. She was a sensitive kid. Lonely and withdrawn when she first came into our lives, the only child of a couple of screwed-up felons who had died separately in tragic and violent circumstances; it had taken a long time for Kerry and me to guide Emily out of her shell, and she still had a tendency, when bad things happened, to retreat into that private little world. She'd been uncommunicative the past two weeks, spending most of her time at home closeted in her room with her computer, her iPod, and Shameless the cat. The cooking and especially the singing were indications that the shell had cracked open and she'd come out into the world again.

She hadn't heard me, because she went right on singing. I shed my coat and hat, tiptoed to the kitchen doorway. Emily's ambition is to become a professional singer and there's no doubt in Kerry's or my mind that she'll succeed one day; she has a clear, sweet voice and tremendous range for a thirteen-year-old with a minimum of vocal training. She can sing anything from folk songs to show tunes—rap and reggae, too, probably, when we're not around to hear her do it. She doesn't need accompaniment and she wasn't using any at the moment; her ears were bare of the iPod buds. I didn't recognize the lyrics or the melody, but what I know about popular music you could put in a disconnected iPod bud.

I stood in the doorway, listening and watching her chop up garlic and onions. And smiling, because she seemed happy again and because I love her as much as if she were my own.

She hit a series of high notes with perfect pitch, finishing the song and the chopping simultaneously, and saw me when she turned from the sink to the stove. She blinked a couple of times, then offered up a shy smile. "Oh, hi, Dad. How long have you been standing there?"

"Long enough. What was that you were singing?"

" 'Pointing at the Sun.' It's a Cheryl Wheeler song."

"I'll bet Cheryl Wheeler doesn't sing it any better than you just did."

She said, "Oh, you're just saying that," but she was pleased.

"If I didn't mean it I'd be fibbing. And you know I don't fib."

"I know. Mom's not home yet—she had to work late. She'll be home around seven."

"She called me, too. What is it you're making there?"

"Vegetarian pasta casserole. We eat too much meat and chicken."

"We do?"

"I think so. Vegetables are a lot healthier."

"Don't tell me you're turning into a vegan?"

"No. Well, maybe. But if I do go vegan, I won't try to convert you and Mom."

"That's good. You can't teach an old carnivore new tricks."

That got me another smile. "Don't worry; you'll like this casserole. You won't even know it doesn't have meat or chicken in it."

Yes, I would. But I said, "Okay. Need any help?"

"No, I . . ." But then she changed her mind and said, "Well, you could put some water on for the pasta."

"Pasta's my speciality."

I got a pot out of the cupboard. Emily went back to the cutting board, to chop up a red bell pepper this time. She didn't do any more singing, but pretty soon she began to hum something up-tempo. Otherwise we worked in companionable domestic silence until the pasta was done and drained and mixed with the vegetables and the casserole was in the oven.

She said then, "Dad? I've been thinking and . . . I'm sorry."

"For what?"

"The way I've been acting since . . . well, you know. It made me so sad and hurt and angry I didn't feel like talking to anybody."

"I understand. You don't have anything to apologize for."

"Well, I just wanted you to know that I'm okay now. I'm not going to think about it anymore."

I went over and put an arm around her and gave her a hug. Good kid, practically an anomaly in these days of rebellious, foulmouthed, drug-experimenting teenagers. Lucky kid, despite all the tragedy in her life.

I hoped Bryn Darby's son had some of the same good fortune. If Bobby was being abused, he was going to need it.

3

JAKE RUNYON

Bryn said, "Bobby has two more bruises, big ones on his left side. He didn't want me to hug him, flinched when I did—that's how I found them."

"How did he explain them?"

"Mumbled something about one of the kids at school punching him. He wouldn't look me in the eye. Jake, I don't know what to do."

Her voice on the phone was low and controlled, but Runyon could hear the angry desperation in it. A faint speech slur, too—she'd been binge drinking lately, nothing but wine but enough of it to feed instead of ease her chronic depression. His fingers were tight around the steering wheel. Outside the car, in the clogged traffic on Upper Market, horns blared and somebody gave somebody else the finger. Typical Friday evening in the city.

"Where's Bobby now?" he asked.

"In his room. He won't talk to me, not about anything."

"You have plans for him tonight or tomorrow?"

"Not tonight. I was going to take him to the Academy of Sciences tomorrow, but . . . I don't know now. Why?"

Runyon didn't usually see her on the weekends when she had her son; his choice, because he didn't want to intrude on their limited time together. But the situation was different now, escalating into critical. "I'd like to come over," he said, "spend a little time with Bobby."

". . . He won't talk to you, either. He hardly knows you."

"He might if I can get him off alone for a while. Man-to-man kind of thing. All right with you?"

"Yes, of course."

"When?"

"Not tonight. Tomorrow morning?"

"I'll be there around eleven."

The weather on Saturday was more of the same that the city had endured all week: cold wind, fog. It would've been easy enough to pick a place to take Bobby if the skies had been clear, but it wasn't a day for the beach or the zoo or Golden Gate Park. An indoor day. The Academy of Sciences was always crowded on weekends—not a good place for a private talk. Besides, there was the problem of convincing the boy to spend time with him alone. He'd need a good reason for that.

He thought of one on the short drive from his apartment to Bryn's home on Moraga Street. A pretty good one that ought to make a nine-year-old cooperative even in his present state.

Bryn's house was brown shingled and, unlike most of the homes in the outer Sunset District, detached from its neighbors. Quiet, middle-class neighborhood whose only drawback was that it was often swaddled in fog. Not much happened there, not until recently anyway. There were always outer Sunset houses for rent at reasonable rates, and some of the city's more enterprising criminals had surreptitiously taken advantage of this and of the fact that most residents minded their own business by establishing both brothels and "grow houses"—marijuana farms complete with irrigation systems and bright lights to simulate sunshine.

The city cops had busted up three active call-girl rings in the area, and federal DEA agents had made nearly a score of busts, most of them small operations but one that had netted eighteen hundred plants plus a large quantity of meth and powdered and crack cocaine. None of this worried Bryn much—she had too many other, more immediate problems to cope with—but it was a source of concern to Runyon. So far all of the illicit activity and subsequent arrests had been nonviolent, but that could change at any time. Where you had crime, especially crime involving drugs, you had the potential for bloodshed.

One more valid reason to legalize and tax the crap out of marijuana and prostitution.

Bryn didn't look well today. Mild hangover coupled with the bitter melancholy that plagued her. She'd been through so damn much—stroke, disfigurement, abandonment by her husband, custody loss of her son, and now this grim new anguish over Bobby's well-being. Dark patches showed like stains beneath a layer of makeup under her eyes. She'd put on dark red lipstick, too, to match the scarf tied across the frozen left side of her face—splashes of bright color more for her son's sake than her own or his, Runyon thought. The red-and-white-checked blouse and green skirt and red ribbon in her ash-blond hair, too.

"Bobby's in his room," she said. "I told him you were coming over, but . . . he doesn't want to go anywhere. If I let him, he'll hide in there all weekend."

"I've got an idea. Tell him I'm here and I'd like to talk to him."

"You won't get anything out of him here. . . ."

"I know. That's not how I'm going to handle it."

Runyon waited in the living room for five minutes. When Bryn came back she said, "All right. But God, he's still so apathetic. He doesn't seem to care about anything."

Bobby's room was at the rear of the house, opposite her office/workroom. Runyon knocked on the door before he stepped inside. The boy was sitting at a small desk, a laptop computer open in front of him; video game images twitched and jumped on the screen and his attention stayed focused on them. He was a gangly kid, tall for his nine years, his brown hair cut in the current short, spiky fashion that made Runyon think of a patch of grass that needed mowing. He wore Levi's and a faded red 49ers sweatshirt with the sleeves cut off. There was a soft cast on his fractured left arm.

Runyon stood by the door, waiting. He didn't want to start this off by pulling adult rank. Bobby was a good kid, shy at the best of times, and generally polite; he wouldn't let too much time go by before acknowledging his visitor.

He didn't. Less than a minute. Then, with reluctance, he shifted his gaze from the screen and said, "Hello, Mr. Runyon," in a small, colorless voice.

"You can call me Jake if you want to."

"I'm not supposed to call adults by their first names."

"Not even if the adult says it's okay?"

". . . I don't know."

"Your mom wouldn't mind. We're good friends, you know."

"I know."

"Jake, then, okay?"

Short silence. Then, "I guess so."

Runyon moved over to where he could see the moving figures on the computer. "What's that you're playing?"

"X-Men," Bobby said. "Children of the Atom."

"Challenging?"

"I guess so."

"Bet you're good at it."

"Sometimes." The boy glanced at the screen again, then clicked off. "Not this time," he said then.

Runyon said, "What I wanted to talk to you about is your mom's birthday. Coming up pretty soon."

"Week after next."

"You have a present for her yet?"

"No. Not yet."

"Know what you're going to get her?"

Bobby shook his head. "I can't think of anything," he said, and paused, and added, "I don't get much of an allowance."

"Well, I'm not sure what to get her, either. I thought maybe you and I could put our heads together, figure out what she'd like."

The boy squirmed a little, not saying anything.

"Drive over to Stonestown," Runyon said, "look around in the stores."

". . . I don't know."

"Don't know if you should? I can fix it with your mom."

Silence. But he was thinking it over.

"I'd really appreciate your help, Bobby. She deserves some nice birthday presents, don't you think?"

"Yes." Then, making up his mind, "Okay, if she says I can go."

"I'll ask her. Give me a couple of minutes."

Bryn was in the kitchen, fiddling with the arrangement of canned goods in a small pantry—make-work while she waited. Runyon said, "So far so good. We're going over to Stonestown, do some shopping."

"Shopping? How'd you manage that?"

"A little psychology."

She stepped out of the pantry and shut the door. "You're good with kids, you know that?"

"Well, I always thought I might be if I had the chance."

She didn't comment on that; she knew what he meant. He'd told her the whole bleak story of his relationship, or lack of one, with his son, Joshua. The mistake he'd made in not fighting harder for custody after he'd filed for divorce from Angela; how she'd taken Joshua away to San Francisco, riddled with vindictive hate and driven by the alcohol dependency that eventually killed her, and convinced him as he was growing up that he was a victim of adultery and careless neglect—neither of which was true. Runyon had never had another chance to be a father—Colleen hadn't been able to have kids—and by the time he'd moved down here from Seattle after Colleen died, it was too late to mend the damage done by Angela's malicious hatred. Joshua wouldn't listen to the truth. He'd called on Runyon once professionally, when his lover was a victim of gay-bashing, but refused to have anything to do with his father since. Unbridgeable gap between them.

Bryn put a hand on his arm. "Be careful with him, Jake. He's very fragile right now."

"I will."

"So am I, for that matter. If I didn't have Bobby . . . and you . . ."

"But you do."

"For now. Sometimes I feel as if I were made of glass. Bump me too hard and I'll shatter into little pieces."

"You're stronger than you think."

"Am I? I don't know." She clutched his arm more tightly. "I can't stand any more of this. It has to stop before it gets any worse."

"It will. We'll put an end to it."

"One way or another," she said.

In the car on the way to the Stonestown mall, Bobby sat fiddling with a berry-colored Game Boy. Runyon let the silence go on until they reached Nineteenth Avenue, then began to do a little probing.

"You like living with your dad, Bobby?"

". . . I guess so, sure." But the words were mumbled and unconvincing.

"Spend a lot of time together with him?"

"Not very much. He works all the time, and I have to . . ."

"Have to what?"

No response.

"What do you do together when he's not working?"

"Not too much. He's always tired, or else . . ."

"Or else?"

No response. The boy's fingers moved rapidly on his computer toy.

"Does he get angry when he's tired? Lose his temper?"

No response.

Runyon tried a different tack. "You know, your mom wishes she could see you more often. She really misses you."

"I know."

"You miss her, too, right?"

Head bob.

"Then how come you stay in your room, instead of spending time with her?"

Six-beat. Then, "I wish it was like it used to be."

"Before your dad moved out?"

"Before she had that stroke. We were a family then."

"The divorce was your dad's idea. He couldn't deal with what happened to her face."

No response.

"It doesn't make any difference to me. Or to you, right?"

Flying fingers, now. "I don't want to talk about this stuff anymore, Mr. Runyon."

"Jake."

No response. And silence the rest of the way to the mall.

Runyon parked in the galleria's underground garage. The mall was enclosed, inhabited by dozens of stores, shops, salons, and cafés on two levels—a few of them empty now, victims of the economic recession. He took Bobby into Macy's, let him wander around looking without making any suggestions.

The boy said nothing until they'd nearly finished making a circuit of the women's clothing department. Then, in that shy way of his, and with a little more animation, "I know what I want to get Mom. But I only have two dollars and it'll cost more than that."

"Tell you what," Runyon said. "I'll loan you the money and you can pay me back out of your allowance. Fifty cents a week or whatever you feel comfortable with."

"My dad wouldn't like that."

"He doesn't have to know, does he?"

"I guess not."

"Just between us. What is it you want to buy?"

Bobby showed him. Good choice. Perfect, in fact, because it was caring, thoughtful, appropriate.

Scarf. Silk scarf.

He spent five minutes making his pick, one unlike any in the collection of scarves Bryn used to cover the nerve-paralyzed side of her face. A deep burgundy color, with an interwoven silver and gold design.

"You think she'll like this one, Jake?"

"I think it'll be her favorite."

Bobby was quiet again on the ride back to the house. But he didn't fiddle with the Game Boy; he sat looking straight ahead, his mouth thinned a little, his forehead ridged. Thinking hard about something.

They were on Moraga, with only a few blocks to go, when Bobby said, "Mr. . . . um, Jake. Are you really a detective?"

"That's right. I was a policeman in Seattle for a long time; now I work for a private agency."

"Do you have a gun?"

"Yes."

"What kind?"

"Three-fifty-seven Magnum."

"Can I see it?"

". . . Why?"

"I've never seen a real gun before."

"Guns aren't toys, Bobby."

"I know that." Pause. "Have you ever shot anybody?"

"Yes. In self-defense."

Another pause. "Could I see it? Please?"

Runyon almost said no, he didn't have it with him. But he didn't like lying, especially to kids. The weapon was locked in the glove compartment, where his permit allowed him to keep it; loaded but with the chamber under the hammer empty. There didn't seem to be any harm in granting Bobby his request.

The house was just ahead. Runyon said as he pulled up in front, "All right, but just a quick look." He shut off the engine, keyed open the glove box. The Magnum was in its clip-on holster; he slid it out, let Bobby have his wide-eyed look.

Runyon was locking the weapon away again when the boy said, "I wish I had a gun like that," in an off-tone that made Runyon glance sharply at him.

"Why? What would you do with it?"

"Keep it for . . . the next time."

"What do you mean, the next time?"

No response.

"The next time your dad hurts you, is that it?"

"My dad doesn't hurt me."

"No? Who, then?"

Silence.

"Who, Bobby?"

The boy's mouth twisted and a name burst out of him,

like a lump of something bitter that he'd hacked up from his throat.

"Francine," he said.

"Who's Francine?"

"I hate her," Bobby said with sudden ferocity, "I hate her, *I hate her!*" And he bolted from the car and raced up the steps to the house.

4

JAKE RUNYON

Bryn came hurrying out to meet him on the porch. "What happened? Why is Bobby so upset?"

"Put a coat on. Let's go for a walk."

"He went running into his room. . . ."

"Better if we talk outside."

Runyon waited until they'd gone a short way to the west, hunched against the fog-threaded ocean wind, Bryn's anxious eyes on him as they walked, before he said, "Do you know anyone named Francine?"

"Francine? The woman Robert's going to marry . . . Francine Whalen. Why?"

In clipped sentences Runyon told her about the gun episode and Bobby's last words before he fled the car.

"Oh my God." Bryn stopped walking, turned to face him. "She's the one who's been hurting him, not Robert. But that's . . . why would she . . ."

"How much do you know about her?"

"Not very much. She's a paralegal, worked for Robert's

43

firm. I didn't like her the first time I met her. The kind of sweetness-and-light type that fool men but not women—a cold, calculating bitch underneath. I think he was sleeping with her before I had the stroke."

"They living together now?"

"Yes."

"Where?"

"He has a flat in the Marina, near the Green. Avila Street."

"Number?"

"Four-sixteen. Upstairs."

"She still working for his firm?"

"No. He's already paying her bills," Bryn said, and then added bitterly, "In exchange for her taking care of Bobby."

"When is the marriage supposed to take place?"

"I'm not sure. Sometime this summer." A wind gust blew up a swirl of discarded fast-food wrappers, but that wasn't what made the visible tremor run through her. She drew her coat collar tight around her throat, held it there with one hand. "I just don't understand any of this. Bobby's silence, for one thing. If Robert was abusing him, yes, but Francine . . . why wouldn't he tell his father, me, somebody?"

"Threats, intimidation. He hates her, but he's also terrified of her."

"But for God's sake why would she hurt a little boy, break his arm, punch him hard enough to leave bruises? She's getting everything she wants . . . Robert, his position, his money."

"No way of telling until we know more about her."

"Whatever the reason, I don't blame Bobby for wishing her dead. I'd like to kill her myself."

"No, you wouldn't."

"Oh yes. Yes, I would."

"That's not the answer, Bryn."

She drew a heavy breath. "What is?"

"Proof," Runyon said. "Solid proof that'll convince your ex, Social Services, the police."

"How do we get it? Bobby? Should I tell him we know Francine's been abusing him?"

"You can try, straight on or roundabout."

"But you don't think he'll admit it?"

"I think he came as close as he could in the car with me."

"Saying how much he hated her . . . that's a cry for help."

"Yes. But in my limited experience with kids, fear always trumps hatred. He's too afraid of the woman and whatever threats she made."

"Damn her! She'll keep right on hurting him, and the next time . . . the next time . . . I won't let it happen. I *won't*."

Runyon said, "There may be something in her background that'll help. I'll see what I can find out. 'Whalen' spelled W-h-a-l-e-n?"

"Yes."

"How old is she?"

"Late twenties, maybe thirty."

"Description?"

"Bottle blonde. Five three or four, slender but top-heavy. Robert always did like big boobs . . . mine weren't enough for him."

Runyon let that pass. "Know anything about her background? Where she was born, if she was married before, has any kids?"

"I think she's divorced, but I'm not sure. I hope to God she never had any children of her own."

"When did she start working for Robert's firm?"

"Three years ago. In the summer."

"Any idea where she worked before?"

"No. Robert never told me and I had no reason to ask."

The good side of Bryn's face was flushed and she was still shivering. Gently he took her arm, turned her back the way they'd come. At the bottom of her porch steps he said, "Better wait awhile before you talk to Bobby, let him calm down."

"Yes."

"Call me afterward."

"I will."

He said, "It'll be all right, Bryn. We'll make it all right." Hollow words and cold comfort, but for now they were all he had to give.

In his apartment on Ortega he brewed a cup of tea and booted up his laptop to run a preliminary background check on Francine Whalen. He wasn't nearly as skilled at computer searches as Tamara, but he'd done enough of them using the agency's search engines and a few of her hacker's tricks to be able to pull up the basics on any known subject.

Finding Francine Whalen proved easy enough. Born in Alameda twenty-nine years ago; father and mother both deceased. Two younger sisters: Gwen, unmarried, a resident of Berkeley, and Tracy, married and living in Ojai in Southern California. Graduate of Sadler Business School in Oakland. Three previous paralegal jobs before joining the West Portal firm of Darby and Feldman three years ago; exemplary references. Married to an S.F. investment banker, Kevin Dinowski, in September 2005; divorced February, 2006, no children. Previous address before moving in with Robert Darby: apartment on Broderick Street in the Laurel Heights neighborhood that she'd shared with another woman, Charlene Kepler, also a paralegal, age twenty-five.

Police record: none, not even a traffic citation.

No red flags in any of that, unless there was something in the brevity of her marriage. Abusers of children were usually one or a combination of three things: victims of abuse themselves, the possessors of deep-seated hostilities and anger management problems, chronic drug users or alcoholics. There was a fourth, less common variety: psychotic child haters, the worst of the lot. Finding out which of these fit Whalen might take some work, but it could be done. The problem was tying whatever explanation for her actions to her abuse of Bobby. Robert Darby, as the boy's legal guardian, was the one who had to be convinced first, and without Bobby's corroboration it'd take conclusive evidence to make his father accept the truth about the woman he was planning to marry.

Runyon did quick checks on her two sisters, ex-husband, and former roommate. Nothing there, either; records all as superficially clean as Francine Whalen's. He created a file of all the information he'd gleaned. If need be, he'd turn it over to Tamara on Monday and ask her to run deeper background checks. One of the benefits, like his talk with Bill yesterday, of working for good people in a small agency.

He spent what was left of the afternoon in front of a bad but commercial-free TV movie. Not watching it, using it for white noise while he waited to hear from Bryn. He had the ability to switch off his thoughts, like shutting down a machine, during any waiting situation. Survival trick he'd learned over the long months of Colleen's illness, the only way he'd been able to keep himself sane and functioning while he watched the cancer eat away at her.

Bryn called a little after six. Her voice was quiet and even toned, but he'd known her long enough to be sensitive to her moods and feelings. As she was to his. Damage control mechanism between two damaged people. He knew what she was going to say before she said it.

"Bobby still won't admit anything, Jake. He won't talk about Francine at all."

"You ask him directly about the abuse?"

"Not at first. I asked how he liked her, if they got along, if he was glad she was going to be his stepmother, that kind of thing. All he did was mumble. He wouldn't look at me the entire time. Finally I just . . . I came right out and asked him if she was hurting him."

"And?"

"That was the only time he reacted. He shouted at me to leave him alone and ran out and hid in the crawlspace."

"Crawlspace?"

"Behind the water heater in the basement. Where he'd go when he was little and something scared him. It took me five minutes to find him and another ten to coax him out." Bryn drew a long, shaky breath, let it out in a faint hiss. "There's no doubt, Jake. He's terrified of that bitch. I came close to getting in the car and driving over to Robert's and confronting her."

"Bad idea," Runyon said. "She wouldn't admit it—and it might make her angry enough to take it out on Bobby."

"I thought of that, too. That's why I didn't do it."

"Don't say anything to your ex, either, when you take Bobby back tomorrow."

"If I take him back."

"Another bad idea if you don't. You know what Robert would do."

"I know, but I can't stand the thought of Bobby being alone with that woman anymore. The next time he does something to provoke her . . . God knows what she might do to him."

Runyon didn't respond. Bryn's fear was legitimate, the point inarguable.

He heard her take another couple of breaths, composing herself. Then she said, "Did you find out anything about Francine?"

"Nothing so far that might explain her behavior. Her marriage didn't last long enough to produce any children."

"Well, thank God for that." Pause. "Jake? Would you try talking to Bobby again tomorrow? He responded so well to you today. . . ."

"Sure. I'll try."

"I hate to keep burdening you with this—"

"It's not a burden. You know I'm there for you."

"Yes. But it seems so one-sided."

"Not so," he said, and meant it. Being there for Bryn meant being there for himself. She was his salvation. Gave him reasons other than work to get up in the morning, ways to fill his days and nights that didn't involve long, aimless, solitary drives. Helped him regain his self-respect. Made him a man again, physically as well as mentally. He wasn't sure whether what he felt for her was love or a kind of abiding gratitude; if it was love, it was an altogether different kind from what he'd shared with Colleen. One thing he did know for certain: he would do anything for Bryn, just as he'd have done anything for Colleen.

He spent part of Sunday afternoon trying to get through to Bobby again. The avuncular approach, the buddy approach, the detective approach. None of it got Runyon anywhere. The boy was locked in tight now, like a frightened young animal hiding in the shadows of a cave. Poking his head out into the light on Saturday had been a onetime thing; he was too afraid to let it happen again.

That left only one way to stop the abuse, the potentially dangerous way—by running a backdoor investigation of Francine Whalen.

5

It didn't take Tamara long to locate Roxanne Lorraine McManus. Just two billable hours, in fact. That kind of speed is good for client relations and PR purposes, but it doesn't do much for the agency's bank account. We weren't going to make much out of the extra document delivery charge, either.

Surprise: Ms. McManus was alive and well and living in San Francisco.

I was in my office where I wasn't supposed to be, doing what I wasn't supposed to be doing, when Tamara brought in the data printout. When I decided to semiretire a few years ago and made her a full partner and essentially turned the agency over to her, the plan was for me to come in a couple of days a week, do a little office work here and there, and pretty much stay out of the field. Yeah, right. Tamara's head for business practices was far superior to mine; in short order she found ways to double our business, which necessitated hiring a second field operative, Alex Chavez, with me taking up the rest of the slack in lieu of hiring a third. Two days a week became three, three became four and sometimes five, and pretty soon I was doing almost as much work as before, office and field both. Some semiretirement. Not that I minded too much, though, most of the time. I've never been any good at sitting around trying to think of something to do with myself, and with Kerry now a vice president at Bates and Carpenter and Emily away at school or off with her friends, the condo was a pretty lonely place on weekdays.

"I'd've found her even sooner," Tamara said, "except that now she's using initials instead of her first and middle names."

"R. L. McManus. Don't find women doing that much."

"Only one I can think of is k d lang."

"I wonder why she made the switch."

"Probably never liked her given names. I wouldn't be too happy with 'Roxanne Lorraine' myself."

"I don't know, I've always thought Roxanne was a pretty name."

"Uh-huh," Tamara said.

I scanned the printout. Computers are fine—I quit being a Luddite where technology is concerned a while ago—but I don't like reading reports, files, or anything else of any length on a monitor screen. Bad for my old eyes, for one thing. But the main reason is that I'm an incurably old-fashioned paper guy. I like the look, feel, and smell of paper in all its many forms. Tamara understands and tolerates this, though she'd be happier if I took up full residence in her techno world and ruined what was left of my eyesight and developed carpal tunnel in the modern fashion.

"Dog-boarding business in Dogpatch," I said. "Woman's consistent in her interests anyway. And she picked the right neighborhood."

"Should've called the business Dogpatch Dog Boarding.

If I had a mutt, I wouldn't take him to a place called Canine Customers."

It wasn't quite as cute as The Warm and Fuzzy Shop but in the same league. Consistent in that respect, too. "Neither would I."

"Doing pretty well, though," Tamara said, "for that kind of business. She's got an A-one credit rating and no outstanding debts. Address is also her residence. Been there nearly seven years on a long-term lease."

"So I see. Must've moved here right after she left Blodgett the second time."

"I can call Alex and have him deliver the stuff from the Catholic Diocese. Or I could drop it off myself after work. Dogpatch isn't far from my new crib."

"No, I'll do it," I said. "I'm out of here when I finish the Bennett report. I'll swing over there on my way home and then notify the client."

Dogpatch is one of the city's smallest and oldest neighborhoods—nine square blocks on the flats east of Potrero Hill (where Tamara's new "crib" was located), one part of it bordering the once-thriving shipyards and mills on the Embarcadero at Pier 70, another part adjacent to recently upscaled Mission Hill. It has a long, rich history dating back to the 1860s, when it was home to thousands of immigrant workingmen and their families. It survived the '06 earthquake and fire pretty much intact, one of the few neighborhoods that weren't devastated, so it's packed with workers' cottages, warehouses, factories, and public buildings a century or more old.

The neighborhood had gotten pretty run-down by the

late seventies, when artists, graphic designers, and other urban professionals discovered it and began the same process of gentrification that was going on in the SoMa district farther north—buying up and renovating its Victorian cottages and Edwardian flats and turning some of the old warehouses into live-work lofts and condos. Nowadays Dogpatch is a diverse mix of historical residences, restaurants and saloons, marine repair outfits, a film company called Dogpatch Studios, the two-block-long American Industrial Center, and the headquarters of the San Francisco chapter of the Hell's Angels.

R. L. McManus's business and residence was on 20th Street, a couple of blocks off Third, the area's main business artery. The house was a renovated and enlarged version of one of the tall, squarish workers' cottages, in good repair and sporting what appeared to be a recent purple and yellow paint job. It sat on a large corner lot, set farther back from the street than its neighbors and bordered by a wrought-iron fence. There were two signs on the fence in front, one on either side of an entrance gate. The larger, professionally lettered one said: *Canine Customers—"A Dog's Home Away from Home."* The smaller, homemade, was more straightforward: *Room for Rent.* A bulky Ford Explorer with tinted windows was parked inside a pair of closed gates; beyond it, at the end of the driveway, I had a partial glimpse of an outbuilding that would be the boarding kennels.

I pushed through the gate, went up onto the porch. Loud barking started up inside as soon as I rang the bell—a pretty large dog, judging from the deep-throated noise. After about five seconds a woman's sharp, commanding voice said, "Quiet,

Thor!" and the yammering cut off instantly in mid-bark. Well-trained animal, the best kind.

The door opened and I was looking at a diminutive woman in her mid- to late thirties with shag-cut blond hair, bright blue eyes, and an even brighter smile. Right age, but not the right woman.

The dog was sitting about a foot behind and to one side of her. A thick-chested, black and brown Rottweiler mix with yellow eyes—hot yellow eyes, like globular flames. The eyes were fastened on me, not exactly as if I were a raw hunk of chateaubriand but not friendly, either.

"Hello," the woman said, making the word seem like a chirp. The bright blue eyes moved over my face in a way that made me think of a supermarket shopper feeling up a piece of fruit to determine its ripeness. "Are you here about the room?"

"No, ma'am. I'm looking for R. L. McManus."

"I'm Jane Carson. If you have an animal you'd like boarded, perhaps I—"

"I'm not a canine customer, either. Is Ms. McManus home?"

The smile lost about half of its candlepower. "What did you want to see her about?"

"Personal business."

"What sort of personal business?"

"I have something for her." I waggled Virden's envelope. "To be delivered personally. It won't take long."

"Your name, please."

I handed her one of my business cards. The woman looked at it, blinked, blinked again, and the smile flattened out into a straight line. She said, "Come in," in a reluctant voice that no longer chirped, and stood aside.

I hesitated, eyeing the Rottweiler.

"Don't worry about Thor," she said. "He's gentle as a lamb."

Sure he was. A were-lamb, maybe. Thor. Some name for a dog. Some dog. But I went in anyway, sidling past him. He didn't move, but his hot yellow gaze tracked me as I trailed Jane Carson across a hallway and into a room that had probably once been a parlor and was now a combination Canine Customers reception office and waiting room. Behind me I heard nails clicking on the hardwood floor as Thor came in after us.

"Wait here, please."

She went away through a door behind a short counter. The Rottweiler sat in a watchful pose, about twelve inches of tongue lolling out of one side of his mouth. I quit looking at him and pretended interest in some of the batch of dog paintings and photographs that covered the walls. I was eyeing a bad watercolor rendering of a mastiff about the size of a small pony when the same door opened and a different woman came in, alone.

R. L. McManus, this time. Not as slender or attractive as she'd been nine years ago, the brunette hair styled differently, cut shorter and waved, her cheeks less rounded and tinted with the kind of waxy shine that comes from more than one facelift done by a plastic surgeon not half as good as the one Kerry had gone to; but the generous mouth and luminous brown eyes hadn't changed much. She was carrying my business card between a blunt thumb and forefinger as if it was something not quite clean. The brown eyes were wary, the cords in her too-smooth neck drawn tight.

"I am Ms. McManus," she said in crisp tones.

"Roxanne Lorraine McManus?"

"I prefer to use my initials. What could a private investigator possibly want with me?"

"It's nothing for you to be alarmed about," I said. "Your ex-husband hired my agency to locate you."

"My ex-husband?"

"David Virden."

There were about five seconds of dead air before she said, "I don't understand. What does he want after all these years?"

"A favor." I extended the envelope. "It's all in here, Ms. McManus. Easier for you to look over the contents than for me to try to explain."

Frowning, she opened the envelope. The frown deepened as she scanned through the Church material; her mouth got tight, loosened and bent a little, then tightened again. "Is this some kind of joke?"

"No, ma'am."

"The Catholic Church can really do this kind of thing?"

"If all the paperwork is in order and the Marriage Tribunal votes in favor."

"And enough money changes hands, I suppose."

I had nothing to say to that.

"Why does he want an annulment now?"

I told her why.

"Well, I think it's ridiculous," she said. "I'd never be a party to anything like this. I want nothing to do with him or the Catholic Church."

"That's your prerogative."

"And don't try to talk me into it."

"Not my job."

"All right, then. Take this back to him and tell him to leave me alone. Don't you bother me again, either."

Her voice had risen slightly, no more than a couple of octaves, but it put the Rottweiler on alert. His ears pricked up and he popped up onto all fours and made a low rumbling sound in his throat, his hot-eyed gaze still fixed on me. The muscles in my shoulders and back bunched. I've had run-ins with dogs before; I don't care how well-trained they are, they can still be unpredictable.

But nothing happened. The woman said, "Quiet, Thor," not as loudly or as sharply as Jane Carson had but with the same effect. The dog subsided immediately, squatting again with that long tongue hanging out.

When she handed me the envelope, I said, "You won't see me again, Ms. McManus. Thanks for your time." And after another detour around Thor, I was out of there.

The day was gray and chilly, but that wasn't the reason for the prickly cold feeling on the back of my neck. Chalk it up to those damn yellow eyes.

In the car I called David Virden's cell number. The call went to his voice mail; I left a brief message, saying that we'd found his ex-wife and asking for an ASAP callback.

It came sooner than I expected, just as I was turning off Third Street onto Army. Never fails. I'm in the car driving and that's when my cell rings. I could let it go to my voice mail, but I'm one of the people who can ignore a ringing phone only in extreme circumstances. Kerry keeps telling me I ought to get one of those Bluetooth things that let you talk on the phone while keeping both hands on the wheel, but I've seen enough drivers who appear to be having animated conversations with themselves and the image is always one of a mental case babbling to a carload of imaginary friends. Better a hands-free device than breaking the law by talking with a phone glued to your ear, as too many people still do despite the recent state law. Or sending text messages or e-mails on laptop computers while driving, two of the crazier techno-surfing, machine-juggling addictions people have been known to indulge in these days.

I'm law-abiding, so I did what I always do, and hardly anybody else seems to, when my cellular goes off: I found a place to pull over and stop and took the call on the fourth ring.

"Fast work finding Roxie," Virden said. "Alive or dead?"

"Alive. Living right here in San Francisco."

"No kidding. Well, that simplifies things, doesn't it."

"No," I said, "it doesn't."

". . . What do you mean? Did you see her, deliver the envelope?"

"I just came from talking to her. She wouldn't take it."

"What? Why the hell not?"

I told him why not.

Long pause this time. Then, hard and angry, "Well, shit! How can she still hate me that much? It's been eight goddamn years."

I had nothing to say to that. Not my area of expertise.

Virden said, "Too bad you didn't find her in a cemetery instead."

Or to that, because it wasn't worth a civil comment.

"She's *got* to sign that document," he said. "It's all that's standing in my way. Nothing else you can do?"

"I'm afraid not."

"Then it's up to me. I don't like the idea of seeing the bitch again, but I'll just have to bite the bullet."

"Do you want us to mail the envelope to you?"

"No. I'll pick it up before I go talk to Roxie. Too late to do it today, I'm meeting Judith at five, and I have a business appointment in the morning. Say one o'clock at your office?"

"Fine. I'll have a report ready for you with her address and the other particulars of the investigation."

"How much more do I owe you?"

"There'll be a final invoice with the other material."

"I'll bring my checkbook." Five or six seconds, and then he said, "Ex-wives. Christ, what a pain they can be."

"I wouldn't know," I said.

"Take my word for it. Even when they're being cooperative, they're a pain in the ass."

Ex-wives weren't the only ones.

6

TAMARA

All day Tuesday, as on most days, she had the office to herself. Bill was out on an interview for an insurance fraud investigation; Jake was following up with the hit-and-run witness. And Alex Chavez was working a pro bono hate-crime case for a black family that was being victimized in Monterey Heights—one more example, as if anybody needed one, that racism was not only alive but running rampant like crap through a sewer.

Fine with her, working alone. She liked being in charge, handling her end of the agency in her own efficient, organized way. Plenty to handle these days, too; business was booming, despite or maybe because of the tanked economy. Two other insurance-related cases, a missing-person investigation, a b.g. check for a rich dude in St. Francis Wood who believed his daughter's brand-new fiancé was after the family fortune . . . plus client reports on closed and in-progress cases, invoices, bookkeeping, and, as a favor to Jake, a deep backgrounder on a woman he suspected of abusing his lady's kid.

All that was liable to keep her here long past five o'clock closing. Had the night before and probably would the rest of the week. Was a time when she'd've chafed at that much over-time because it cut into what little social life she had. Now, she welcomed it. After what'd happened a couple of weeks ago, being alone in the office was a lot more comfortable than holing up alone in her flat on Potrero Hill. The flat just didn't feel the same as it had when she moved in. Maybe never would again. But she was stuck there for another ten months, like it or not; the lease was ironclad and she'd lose a bundle if she broke it. Besides, she was just too busy to go hunting for another place to live.

Antoine Delman, aka Lucas Zeller. That son of a bitch. Nearly ruined her life . . . nearly *took* her life. Not enough time had passed for her to get over her outrage every time she thought about him and what he'd tried to do to her and a whole long list of other brothers and sisters. Happiest day coming up was the one she'd spend in court testifying against him and his freaky mama.

Something else he'd done to her was sour her on men. The way she felt right now, she didn't care if she ever had another relationship, ever even got laid again. Use it or lose it? Well, maybe it was better to lose it than risk losing everything else because of it.

The morning went by quickly, with only one phone call to interrupt her work. Just after one o'clock the annulment cli-ent, David Virden, showed up to collect his envelope and the report she'd typed out for him. He didn't look at the report, just asked her if his ex-wife's current address was in it. Well, of course it was; what did he think they'd do, hide it from him? He didn't look at the invoice, either. Demanded to know what he owed, wrote a check for the full amount, and stalked out without bothering to say thanks or good-bye. Mr. Personality. No wonder none of his first three marriages had lasted. Another of those slick dudes, like that bastard Antoine, who were all surface charm when they wanted something or somebody, but cut them open and what you'd find inside was a mess of dirty ice and a festering ego.

Tamara had most of her priority client work caught up by two thirty. Which left reports and bookkeeping, neither of which she felt like tackling just yet. Instead she started in on the deep backgrounder for Jake. Child abuse was about as low a crime as there was; anything she could do to help put a stop to what was happening to Bryn's son was a mandate.

Francine Whalen. Jake had been fairly thorough in what he'd pulled up on the woman so far, but the Net was a vast storehouse of information, some of it distorted and useless, and what you had to do was get down into the nooks and crannies far below the surface and then start a careful sifting. Same principle as rummaging around in attics and sub-basements and dusty old buildings where the long-stored, valuable stuff was hidden away.

Didn't have much luck at first. The twenty-nine years of Whalen's life to date seemed pretty clean, without any apparent psychological or other problems. Except for the five-months-and-out marriage to the investment banker, Kevin Dinowski, but that could've been simple incompatability; whatever the reason for the quick split, there was no indication of it in the public record. Still, everybody had some dark spots in their lives, no matter how small or how well buried. Get a hint of what they were and you could usually pull them out into the open.

Tamara picked up the Whalen hint when she started probing into the lives of her two sisters. Gwen Whalen, the unmarried one living in Berkeley, had tried to commit suicide when she was sixteen and had spent three months in a psychiatric facility. Wasn't her only stay in a twitch bin—six months in another at age twenty. No public record on cause or treatment in either case, and hacking into private hospital files was a risky proposition; get caught and there went your career down the rabbit hole. The last of Gwen's two incarcerations was six years ago; she seemed to have pulled her life together since then. The past several years she'd worked as a caregiver in a Berkeley elderly-care facility called the Sunshine Rest Home and, from all indications, appeared to be leading a normal life. What passed for one these days, anyhow.

Tracy Holland, the second, married sister living down in Ojai, had one stand-out blemish on her record: arrested four years ago for battery on her six-year-old daughter, the charge brought by her mother-in-law. Charge was dropped the next day, either because the mother-in-law changed her mind or because Tracy's husband had stepped in on her behalf. Social Services had looked into the matter, but they must not have found anything to justify taking further action. The Hollands were still married, still had custody of the child.

Broad hints, both of these. When kids were abused, they often developed one kind of psychological problem or another as they got older, and some of them turned into abusers themselves when they became parents. So if all three Whalen girls had been childhood victims of abusive parents, that might be the answer to why a childless woman like Francine would start beating up on the first kid to come into her charge.

One problem with that idea: the girls' parents weren't the likeliest of suspects. The father, George Whalen, had died in a freak industrial accident when Francine, the oldest of the girls, was five and the youngest, Gwen, just two. Pretty young for abuse to start . . . unless he'd been one of these real sickos who get off on sexually and physically molesting their kids when they're barely out of infancy. Could also have been the mother, after the father was dead, taking out her frustrations on her daughters—that kind of thing happened often enough—but Arlene Whalen had been in declining health for years with a blood disease that finally took her out when Francine was thirteen. Neither George nor Arlene had any kind of police record, and there were no red flags in their personal or professional lives.

After Arlene's death, the girls had been raised by her mother in Grandma's home in Concord. Another possibility there. The grandmother, Joan Cartwright, had been in her mid-sixties, widowed and living alone for eight years, when she took the kids in. Figure her quiet life had to've been disrupted by the presence of three young girls and the hassles of coping with them. Possible she'd taken out *her* frustrations by using them as punching bags.

Tamara did some probing into Joan Cartwright's life. Nothing there to support the theory. So then she went back and dug deeper into Francine Whalen's, as deep as she was able to without a lead in a new direction, but all she got out of that was an empty hole.

Well, the sisters-abuse angle was something, at least, for Jake to follow up on. She got him on his cell, caught him free, and laid out what she'd learned and the possibilities it indicated. Nothing more she could do for him now.

Time to bite the bullet, get to work on the backlog of reports and bookeeping. But the phone, which had been silent most of the day, kept ringing to interrupt her. Three calls in the space of half an hour, the first two expected and routine: Bill checking in, then Alex checking in. It was the third call and the reason for it that surprised and rocked her.

"This is David Virden. What the hell's the matter with you people?" Angry, real angry. "One simple little job and you go and screw it up, make me look like a fool. How could you make such a stupid mistake?"

"What're you talking about?"

"Finding my ex-wife, what do you think I'm talking about. Christ, no wonder that woman wouldn't take the goddamn envelope."

"What woman?"

"The dog-boarding McManus," Virden said. "Her initials might be the same, she might look a little like Roxie, but she's *not* my ex-wife. I never saw that woman before in my life."

7

JAKE RUNYON

He was in the East Bay, done with interviewing a second witness in the hit-and-run case whose name had been provided by the first one he'd tracked down, when Tamara called. He'd intended to talk to Francine Whalen's ex-husband before the sister in Berkeley, but since he was in the general vicinity, and given what Tamara had uncovered, Gwen Whalen was a better choice. If there was a history of abuse in the Whalen girls' childhood, it might explain Francine's behavior toward Bobby. Convincing anyone to admit to that kind of thing, particularly a woman who'd spent time in mental hospitals, was liable to be difficult. Depended on how close Gwen was to her sister, their joint history. The fact that she worked as a caregiver likely meant she had compassion, a sense of mercy. Work on that angle if he could.

Tamara had provided phone numbers. He called the Sunshine Rest Home first; Gwen Whalen's shift had ended at four, he was told. The facility was in northeast Berkeley, at the edge of the hills near the Albany line, and her apartment was several miles away, on the southwest side of the university. It took Runyon forty minutes to drive there from Union City.

Four-unit apartment building, old and drab, on a street of similar dwellings. Probably a mixture of off-campus housing for U.C. students and relatively inexpensive rentals for moderate-income members of the workforce like Gwen Whalen. Her apartment was number two, first floor rear. She lived alone, apparently; G. Whalen was the only name on the mailbox.

No answer any of the three times he rang the bell. But now that he was here, he was reluctant to leave. Give it a while. Could be she'd stopped to run an errand or two on her way home.

He'd had to park two blocks away, and lucky to get a space that close; Berkeley's residential streets were always jammed, particularly the ones close to major arteries like this neighborhood was to Ashby. No point in going back to the car to wait, so he walked it off. Ten blocks one way, ten blocks back to ring Gwen Whalen's bell again. He did this three times, killing most of another hour, before he finally got a response.

The intercom was ancient and in poor repair; he could barely understand the woman's voice that came through it amid hiccuping bursts of static. She must've had the same problem, kept saying, "What?" each time he spoke, so that he had to repeat himself. Name, profession—shortening it to "investigator"—and a request for a brief interview on a personal matter. The intercom went silent. And again he waited. Maybe she'd buzz him in; maybe she wouldn't.

She didn't, but she did come to peer at him through a peephole in her door. When he heard heavy steps approaching, he opened the leather case containing the photostat of his license. Let her take a good look at him, then held the license up next to his face and close to the peephole.

Close to a minute went by before she said, "What do you want with me?" The words were slightly muffled by the door, but the wariness in them came through clearly enough.

"Personal matter involving a client."

"What client? What personal matter?"

"Her name is Bryn Darby. The case involves her son."

"I don't know anyone named Bryn Darby."

That told him something right there. "My investigation has nothing to do with you specifically, Ms. Whalen. I only have a few questions—I won't take up much of your time."

Another minute ticked away. Thinking it over, making up her mind. Curiosity tipped the decision in his favor, as it often did in situations like this. A pair of locks clicked in succession; the door opened partway on a chain. The face that peered out through the gap was moon round, topped by a loose pile of dark, curly hair.

"My neighbors are home," she said.

Not as much of a non sequitur as it might seem. Runyon understood: she was telling him that if he made any kind of false move, all she had to do was scream and somebody would come running.

"Be easier if we talk inside. If you don't mind."

She thought that over, too, but not for long. The door closed, stayed closed for ten seconds or so as if she was still uncertain; then the chain rattled and she opened up. And immediately retreated a few steps and stood in a nervously defensive posture, her hands fisted under heavy breasts, as he stepped inside.

Big woman, bulging shapelessly in a set of pale green scrubs. Not quite morbidly obese, but edging up on it. The round face might have been pretty if it weren't for the bloated jowls, the folds of flesh under her stub of a chin. The fat rolls had a soft, puffy-pink look, the color of a baby's skin.

"I don't like to be stared at," she said.

"I meant no offense, Ms. Whalen. Studying people I meet for the first time is part of my job."

He shut the door. They were in a longish hallway palely lit by a single globe; a more brightly lit room was visible at the far end. Two odors dominated among the mingled smells: the ghosts of hundreds of fried-food meals, and Lysol disinfectant.

She said, plucking at a sleeve, "These are my work clothes. I just got home, I haven't had time to change."

"I admire people who work as caregivers."

"How did you— Oh. I suppose you know all about me."

"Not really. A few basic facts."

"What happened when I was nineteen? And afterward?"

"Yes."

It was the right answer. She said, "I don't make a secret of any of that. It's part of my therapy to be open about it. Not that I go around broadcasting it, but if someone already knows . . ." She plucked at her sleeve again, turned abruptly, and waddled down the hallway, casting looks back over her shoulder to see how closely Runyon was following.

The lit room was a good-sized living room, clean and tidy to a fault, nothing out of place. The furniture was old but of decent quality. On one wall hung a large, painted-wood crucifix, the colors so vivid the blood on Christ's hands and feet seemed almost real; there were no pictures, no other adornments. Through partly drawn drapes and mullioned windows Runyon could see portions of a small backyard.

Gwen Whalen turned toward him again. In the brighter light he saw that her deep-sunk eyes were brown and moist— gentle eyes. And now that her wary suspicion had dimmed, the emotions reflected in them were uncomfortably familiar. Pain, loneliness. The same things he saw when he looked into Bryn's eyes; that had stared back at him for too long whenever he looked into a mirror. Another damaged soul.

She said, "I'm going to have some chocolate milk. I have coffee and tea, too, but no alcohol."

"Nothing for me, thanks."

She went into an adjacent kitchen, came back with a plate of chocolate-chip cookies and an oversized, napkin-wrapped tumbler poured to the brim. "Aren't you going to sit down?"

"Yes, thanks."

She waited until he sat on one of a pair of Naugahyde chairs, then lowered herself onto a matching couch and set the plate on a low table between them. One of the cookies went down in three bites, followed by half the chocolate milk in a series of gulping swallows that left her with a slick brown mustache.

"I haven't eaten since noon," she said, "nothing except two Butterfingers. If I don't get something in my stomach, I start to feel sick."

"I understand."

She ate another cookie, drank the rest of the milk, and carefully wiped off the upper-lip residue with the napkin. "I haven't always been this fat," she said then. "I was just the opposite in high school, almost anorexic. I started eating too much after I got out of the hospital the first time, when I tried to kill myself."

"Why did you want to end your life?"

"The doctors said it was low self-esteem, a lack of direction and purpose. I guess that's true. I was sad and unhappy and just . . . you know, drifting."

"Why? Difficult childhood?"

A vein bulged and pulsed on one temple. It was several seconds before she said, "Yes. Difficult."

"In what way?"

"I didn't care about anything," she said, not answering the question. "I just wanted to die. That's what I thought then, anyway."

"But now you think differently."

"Yes, but it took a long time. I was still sick after they let me out of the hospital. Not so bad that I wanted to die anymore, but I had to go back again later for more therapy before I was finally cured."

"Cured by the therapy?"

"That, and finding work I cared about, my purpose in life—helping people who are worse off, who need me. I found Jesus, too. He really helped a lot." She looked up at the crucifix, smiled, and reached for another cookie.

Runyon said, "Do you mind if I ask you a personal question?"

"Well, I've been telling you personal things, haven't I."

"Are you close to your sisters?"

The cookie stopped moving a couple of inches from her mouth. "My sisters?"

"Francine in particular."

"Why do you want to know that?" Tense all of a sudden,

the hurt in her eyes magnified and joined by some other emotion that Runyon couldn't quite identify. Fear, maybe.

"The reason I'm here," he said. "Bryn Darby and her son."

"I told you, I don't know anyone named Bryn Darby."

"Francine does. You know she's engaged to be married?"

". . . No, I didn't know."

"You're not close, then. Don't communicate often."

"No. I haven't seen her in . . ." She dammed up the rest of what she'd been about to say by shoving the entire cookie into her mouth. Ate it so fast, glancing up again at the crucifix, that crumbs dribbled out unchecked; she choked on one of the swallows and that started a spate of coughing. Her face was a mosaic of pink and dark red splotches.

Runyon watched her get the coughing under control, dab at her mouth with the napkin, then begin picking the crumbs off her lap one by one and depositing them on the plate. At length he asked, "Why don't you get along with Francine, Ms. Whalen?"

"I don't have to answer that." Not looking at him, still picking crumbs.

"No, you don't. So you don't care that she's engaged."

"Why should I? She doesn't care about me."

"What about your other sister?"

"Tracy? Francine doesn't care about her, either."

"But you do?"

"Yes, but she lives in Southern California. We talk on the phone sometimes, but I haven't seen her in . . . I don't know, a long time." Gwen Whalen's head came up. "Why are you asking me all these questions? What do my sisters have to do with Bryn Darby and her son?"

Runyon said, "The man Francine is engaged to is Bryn's ex-husband, Robert Darby. They live together in San Francisco."

"Living together before marriage is a sin."

"The boy lives with them—he's nine years old. The father has custody."

Her eyes rounded. "Nine?" she said.

"Francine takes care of him while the father works. The boy doesn't like her. His mother thinks he's afraid of her, that he has good reason to be."

"Oh, my Lord!"

"Can you tell me why a little boy would be afraid of your sister?"

"No!" Neither a negative response nor a denial, but a cry of anguish. "No, no, no!"

"He has a fractured arm, bruises—"

"Don't tell me; I don't want to hear it!" She heaved to her feet, stood spraddle legged with her hands in front of her, palms outward, as if warding off an attack. Her gaze was back on the crucifix. "O Jesus, look down in mercy. Forgive our sins, forgive those who have sinned against us."

"Francine hurt you and Tracy, didn't she? When you were growing up."

Violent headshake.

"Please tell me. I need to know."

"Holy Mary, Mother of God, pray for us sinners now and at the hour—"

"For the boy's sake. To keep him from being hurt anymore."

She backed up, still shaking her head. Stumbled against a corner of the couch and staggered off-balance—would have fallen if Runyon hadn't come up fast out of his chair and caught her arm to steady her. There was a gathering hysteria in her face, the whites of her eyes showing. She wrenched free of him, cringing, as if his touch terrified her.

"You have to leave now. You have to leave. Go away, go away, *go away!*"

There was nothing he could do but comply. And in a hurry. If he'd lingered, he felt sure she would have started screaming.

8

I was home watching a Discovery Channel special on sea otters with Emily when Tamara called on my cell. Not the Seriously Adult Tamara this time, Furious Tamara, one I'd only met a few times, and glad of it. Spitting so much fire I could almost feel the blistering heat coming over the phone wire.

It took a few seconds to straighten out what she was saying. "R. L. McManus isn't Virden's ex-wife? That's what he told you?"

"Claimed we made a mistake. Said we were incompetent. Said he was stopping payment on his checks and taking his business to another agency."

"What'd you say to him?"

"Not what I felt like saying. Told him I hadn't made a mistake, has to be another explanation, but the man wouldn't listen. Said he ought to know his ex when he saw her, even after eight years, and hung up on me."

"Can't argue with that. The part about him knowing his ex when he saw her—"

"Don't you start telling me I screwed up."

"I wasn't going to. You don't make that kind of mistake."

"Damn straight I don't. Not on a simple trace, not on *any* trace with as much starter info as that dude handed you. Just to make sure, I double-checked. Everything says R. L. Mc-Manus is Virden's first wife."

I thought back to the few minutes I'd spent with the woman. "I asked her if she was Roxanne Lorraine McManus and she didn't deny it, just said she preferred to use her initials. She didn't deny Virden was her ex-husband, either . . . though come to think of it, she didn't offer any confirmation."

"Can't be two women with that name, or I'd've turned it up. And Virden wouldn't have any reason to lie, right? He says she's not his ex, then she's not."

"Despite the resemblance. Right."

"Well, then? Tell you the same thing it tells me?"

"Identity theft," I said.

"Yeah. Whoever that Canine Customers bitch is, she's passing as the real Roxanne McManus and has been for the past seven years."

I'd taken the phone out into the kitchen; I made two passes back and forth, thinking it out. Identity theft is a huge crime problem these days, with staggering numbers of victims nationwide—something like twelve million the previous year and that number rising annually by double-digit percentage points. Most of the cases were low-tech and committed for quick profit, but there were plenty of incidents of individuals whose entire lives had been taken over—and sometimes ended—by identity thieves. Only a few of the cases we'd handled to date had involved that type of scam, none of them major, but I knew someone who'd had a hellish personal experience with one—Sharon McCone, good friend and fellow investigator, in a high-profile case a few years back.

I said, "The real McManus was last seen in Blodgett, before she moved away to go into business with a friend she'd just met. You turn up anything along those lines?"

"Nothing. So maybe the friend's the look-alike thief?"

"Maybe. If it was a woman."

"Well, whoever the impostor is, she must've done away with the real McManus. Nobody falls off the radar for seven years if they're still aboveground."

"Don't get ahead of yourself," I said. "Could be a case of swapped identities. That kind of thing happens now and then."

"Yeah, well, what do we do now? Can't just let it slide."

"See what you can find out about the other woman at Canine Customers, Jane Carson. We owe the client that much follow-up."

"Not if he stops payment on his checks we don't."

"I'll try to talk him out of that. Once he understands we're not at fault, he may be more reasonable."

"Wouldn't bet on it. Probably hang up on you like he did on me."

"One step at a time. Or don't you want to run the Carson check?"

"Sure I do. Won't do our rep any good unless we find out what's going on here."

"Okay then."

"And when we do find out? Notify the law?"

"Not our call without definite proof of fraud. Up to Virden if he wants to pursue it."

"Better get in touch with him right away," she said, "let

him know what we suspect. And don't forget about his stop-payment threat."

"Yes, boss."

That got me a sardonic little chuckle. Furious Tamara was all through venting; Seriously Adult Tamara was back in the saddle. "I'll be in the office awhile, you want to call me back."

"As soon as I talk to Virden," I said.

Only I didn't talk to Virden. My call to his cell went straight to voice mail. I left an urgent call-back message, but it didn't get returned.

Tamara had another surprise for me when I walked into the agency Wednesday morning. She came out of her office while I was shedding my overcoat and said without preamble, "This McManus thing gets weirder and weirder. Far as I can find out, the other woman doesn't exist."

"What other woman?"

"Jane Carson. City business license for Canine Customers lists R. L. McManus as sole owner and operator, no employees. Real estate outfit that handles the lease doesn't have any record of a Jane Carson living at the Twentieth Street address, and neither does any other source."

"So she could be living somewhere else."

"Uh-uh. Lot of Jane Carsons in the city and the Bay Area, and none of 'em match."

"Could be she recently moved here from out of state, hasn't been here long enough to trace."

"That'd make her a new hire then, right?"

"Or a new roomer. McManus rents out rooms, with or without the property owner's knowledge and permission; there's a sign on the fence in front."

"Carson's not either one," Tamara said. "You told me she handled that Rottweiler like a pro. Can't just walk in off the street and take over handling a big trained watchdog. Takes time, plenty of patience. Woman has to've been working or living there for weeks, if not months."

I conceded the point.

"So if her real name's Jane Carson and she's had experience with dogs, I should've been able to get a hit on her on one of the real-time sites. Wasn't even a hint."

"So you think it's an assumed name?"

"Or else there're two identity thieves in that house."

"Possible, but we don't want to make any judgment leaps here. Or get too deeply involved without client sanction. Besides, there's a catch in the scenario we've been building up."

"What catch?"

"The profit motive. I can see an opportunist stealing the real Roxanne McManus's ID in order to lay hands on the money she got from the sale of her pet shop seven years ago. But then why use it to lease a house here in the city, start up a dog-boarding business, and continue to live as McManus? She can't be making that much out of Canine Customers."

"Maybe she's got herself a sideline."

"You didn't find any record of one."

"Wouldn't be a record if it was something illegal."

"Then why is she supplementing her income by renting out a room or rooms? It doesn't add up."

Tamara admitted grudgingly that it didn't seem to.

"How much is the monthly nut on her lease?" I asked.

"Thirty-five hundred. Cheap for property that size—some new loft apartments in the neighborhood are renting for that much—but still a lot of green."

"More than you and I could afford. Factor in utilities, food, general expenses, and she has to be laying out a minimum of six thousand a month. Where's the money coming from?"

"Yeah, where?"

"How much did the Blodgett pet shop sell for, do you know?"

"No, didn't seem important at the time. But I'll find out."

"Small business in a little town near the Oregon border—couldn't've been a large amount."

"Might be enough to explain the original ID theft. Phony McManus could've talked her into selling."

"The whole thing still seems off to me. Why would she use stolen money to move here, lease a house, and then spend seven years as a dog boarder and room renter?"

"Could've had some cash of her own."

"Then why not set herself up in a better location, and in a more lucrative business?"

Tamara said, "Maybe she's not greedy. Just wanted a house, enough income to live the way she wants."

"Identity theft is a hell of a risk to run for that kind of return."

"Doesn't explain where this Jane Carson fits in, either. Damn."

I said, "Find out the sale price on the pet shop. I'll see if I can get hold of Virden."

"Funny he didn't return your call."

"Not if he was as angry as you said he was."

In my office I put in a call to Virden's cell number. Out of Service message, this time. His place of business was Hungerford and Son, a San Jose firm that manufactured parts for washers, dryers, and other large appliances; the Hungerford number was on the card he'd given me. The woman who answered there said Mr. Virden was out of the office today and she didn't know where he could be reached.

He'd handwritten both his cell and residence numbers on the back of the card, so I tried the home one. Answering machine. Well, hell. I left a similar message to the one on his voice mail last night, stressing the importance of a callback ASAP.

Tamara came in through the connecting door. "Ten thousand for the pet shop," she said.

"About what I figured. Enough to make an initial ID theft worthwhile, but that's about all. Unless the real McManus had other assets—a trust fund, something like that."

"She didn't. I checked first time around."

"What about the aunt? Money of her own, maybe a large insurance policy with her niece as beneficiary?"

"Checked on that, too. No. Owns a small house in Blodgett, worth about fifty K. Lives on Social Security. No life insurance."

"So we could be on the wrong track after all," I said. "Looking for a felony where none exists."

"You think? I don't. Why's this Dogpatch woman pretending to be Roxanne McManus if she's not an ID thief? And what happened to the real Roxanne? And what's up with Jane Carson?"

"Good questions. Maybe the answers are simple, not sinister, and we just haven't thought of them yet."

"Balls," she said.

"Well, in any case, we're on hold until I talk to Virden. No client, no ongoing investigation."

"Don't have to tell me. I learned that lesson the hard way."

Nothing from Virden by close of business. I tried his cell one more time, got the same Out of Service message.

"Still pissed and ducking us," Tamara said.

"Probably. I'll make one more try tomorrow."

"What do we do if he's blown us off?"

"You know the answer to that. Mark the case closed and forget about it. There's nothing else we can do."

9

JAKE RUNYON

Getting people to talk about their private lives was never easy, and a subject as delicate as child abuse made the job twice as difficult. If they were willing to talk at all, emotions flared up and got in the way: lies, evasions, exaggerations, angry recriminations, irrational outbursts like the one from Gwen Whalen. That was one common reaction; the other was the one he'd gotten from the other sister, Tracy, when he reached her by phone in Ojai. As soon as he mentioned Francine's name, Tracy said in bitter tones, "I have nothing to say about her," and hung up on him. Either way, a refusal to cooperate. The fact that Francine had two estranged sisters, one of whom had suffered severe emotional damage, was significant to him, but it wouldn't be to Robert Darby. Lawyers were a breed apart. You had to practically hit them over the head with hard evidence, and even then they were liable to twist its interpretation to meet their own ends.

Late Tuesday afternoon he went to see Francine's ex-husband, Kevin Dinowski, at the California West Exchange

Bank downtown. Dinowski had an impressive-sounding title, Regulatory Market Risk Representative, but judging from the size of his windowless office, it was neither a high-level nor a high-paying position. Runyon got in to see him by using the "personal matter" approach; few people were able to resist when a private investigator had that kind of interest in them—assuming they had nothing to hide.

Dinowski was in his thirties, enthusiastic, and friendly enough until Runyon mentioned Francine's name. Then he stiffened and pulled back. But he didn't close off. Bitterness and something that might have been hatred for his ex-wife made him willing to talk about her. You could almost see the professional poise peeling away like layers of dead skin, to reveal the private scars and still-open wound underneath.

"What's she done now?" he said.

"Now, Mr. Dinowski? She do something before?"

"Soured me on marriage, for one thing."

"I understand you were married only a short time."

"I must've been out of my mind," Dinowski said. "Blinded by sex, that's my only excuse. It's true what they say—you don't really know someone until you live with them for a while."

When he didn't go on, Runyon prompted him with, "We all make mistakes."

"Some bigger than others. I'll never make one like Francine again."

"Another man is about to. She's engaged to be married."

"Well, I feel sorry for the poor guy, whoever he is. Is that why you're here? Checking up on her for her future husband?"

"Something like that. He has a little boy, nine years old, from a previous marriage."

"Francine as a wife is bad enough, but as a mother? I pity that kid."

"Why?"

"Because she's crazy, that's why. Ceritifiable."

"How is she crazy?"

Dinowski looked away, not answering. A muscle fluttered along his jaw. The shape of his mouth was lipless, pinched.

Runyon said, gambling, "Violent tendencies?"

"Tendencies? She's psychotic when something sets her off, and it doesn't take much to set her off." Dinowski shot the left sleeve of his suit coat, unbuttoned his shirt cuff, and drew that up. The skin along his forearm bore a long puckered scar. "See this? She threw a pot of boiling water at me one night. Just because of a mild criticism of what she was cooking. If I hadn't ducked away in time, it'd be my face that's scarred. That was the last straw. The next day I filed for divorce."

"There were other incidents, then?"

"Oh yes. None as bad as the boiling water, but bad enough. Just fly into a rage for no good reason. One time in bed she . . . never mind the details. It was the only time I ever hit her, slapped her, and she scratched the hell out of me in return. Lord, I wish I'd never laid eyes on her. Those were the worst five months of my life."

"Would you be willing to repeat what you've just told me, Mr. Dinowski?"

"Repeat it? To whom?"

"Her fiancé, the father of the little boy I told you about."

"To stop Francine from marrying him, is that it?"

Runyon said, "There's a chance she may have been taking out her aggressions on the boy."

"Christ. Hurting him, you mean?"

"He has a fractured arm and multiple bruises."

"A nine-year-old kid? Well, I'm not really surprised. I told you she was crazy, totally out of control."

"Can I count on your cooperation, then?"

"Cooperation?" Dinowski hesitated. Wary thoughts had come into his head; Runyon could tell by his body language and the sudden altered state of his expression. "I don't know. If I step into this, spoil her plans, she's liable to come after me again. I wouldn't put anything past her."

"You'd be saving the boy a lot more grief."

"Or causing him more. She could take it out on him, too, you know. This man she's marrying . . . who is he? Somebody important? Somebody with money, I'll bet. Francine loves money."

"He's a family law attorney."

"A lawyer? Wait a minute, now. I can't afford to get involved with lawyers. My position here at the bank, my finances . . . a lawsuit would ruin me . . . no. No, I don't think I'd better get involved."

"Think about the boy, Mr. Dinowski—"

"No, I'm sorry. No. I'd like to help, but it's not my problem; *she's* not my problem anymore. I shouldn't have said anything to you in the first place." He drummed blunt, nervous fingers on the desktop. "You're not going to repeat it to this lawyer, are you? Without my permission?"

"Not without permission, no."

"Well, good, I appreciate that. I wouldn't want it to get back to Francine. As crazy as she is, there's no telling what she might do. You understand, don't you? I hope you find some other way to stop her from marrying the lawyer, hurting the boy anymore, I really do—"

Runyon was on his feet by then and moving toward the door. He left without giving Kevin Dinowski another glance or another word.

Francine Whalen's ex-roommate, Charlene Kepler, still lived in the same apartment on Broderick Street in Laurel Heights. Runyon drove out California Street from downtown, but he didn't go directly to the Broderick address. It was not quite five o'clock, and Charlene Kepler wasn't likely to be home yet; she worked for an insurance company in the Transamerica building.

He turned into the Laurel Heights shopping center. You could find a Chinese restaurant in just about any mall in the city, and this one was no exception. He'd eaten Chinese food five or six times a week after Colleen was gone; it had been her favorite and he'd used it as a way to maintain a connection to her and the life they'd shared together. He hadn't felt the need as often since meeting Bryn, but it was what he was in the mood for tonight. Chinese restaurants were usually quiet and orderly, good places to think as well as eat.

Over tea and a plate of kung pao chicken and fried rice, he went over his talk with Kevin Dinowski. As much as Dinowski seemed to hate Francine, he might've exaggerated the extent of her behavior, but that scar on his arm, assuming he'd gotten it the way he claimed he had, said otherwise. Further confirmation that Francine was violence prone and unstable. Capable of greater acts of violence than hurling a pot of boiling water, inflicting bruises, and breaking a little boy's arm. Capable of killing someone, child or adult, if one of her sudden rages got amped up high enough and she completely lost control.

Runyon had already decided not to repeat what Dinowski had told him to Bryn. Without the self-centered banker's cooperation, it would only increase her fear and anxiety.

Dinowski, out. Francine's two sisters, out. Maybe Charlene Kepler had a horror story of her own to tell and was willing to pass it on to Robert Darby. But even if she did, there was no guarantee it would do any good. Without a second or third person's account to back it up, Darby might claim she had an ax to grind and dismiss it as fabrication. A man in love or lust, a man who had yet to be subjected to Francine's violent outbursts, was a man in denial.

Runyon had lost his appetite, not that he'd had much to begin with. He left half the meal unfinished, went back out into the foggy night.

Charlene Kepler was home and willing enough to talk to him. Runyon interviewed her in an untidy living room while her current roommate banged pots, pans, and dishes in the kitchen. Kepler was a plump thirtyish redhead, the chattery, scatterbrained type who had an annoying habit of starting every other sentence with "well" and sprinkling others with "you know."

"Well, I don't know what I can tell you about Francine," she said. "We were roomies for only about five months and that was, what, six or seven years ago. I haven't seen her since she moved out to get married."

"So you weren't close friends?"

"Well, no, we weren't. We shared expenses and that's about it."

"How did you happen to get together?"

"Well, we were both working at the same place, Mitchell

and Associates—that's a law firm in Cow Hollow. I was in the secretarial pool and she was one of the, you know, the paralegals. Well, she'd been living with this guy and they broke up because he got another job back east someplace and she needed a place to live. And I needed a roommate because the girl I was living with moved out to get married. My roomies are always moving out to get married, I don't know what it is—I wish I had that luck with *my* relationships. Well, anyway, that's how we got together."

"The guy Francine was living with—do you remember his name?"

"Well, no, not exactly. David, Darren, something like that."

"Last name?"

"I don't think she ever mentioned it."

"Did she say what kind of work he did, where his new job was?"

"Well . . . no, I don't think so. She didn't talk about him much. I mean, well, you know how it is when you break up with somebody; you don't want to even *think* about the person."

"How did you and Francine get along?"

"Oh, well, okay, I guess. We didn't spend very much time together. She had her life and I had mine."

"Ever have any problems with her?"

"Problems? You mean did we argue or fight about stuff?"

"Yes."

"Well, there were a few times. She liked everything neat and tidy and I'm not a neat and tidy person. I mean I try not to be a slob, but I just don't care about picking up after myself, you know? Life's too short to worry about the little things."

"Did she ever become violent?"

Kepler blinked at him as if he'd asked her a question in a foreign language she didn't understand.

Runyon said, "I've been told that Francine has a violent temper, a tendency to lose control when she's angry. Did she ever attack you, try to hurt you?"

"Well . . ." The plump face colored slightly. Kepler's voice was rueful when she said, "Well, there was one time, right before she moved out. She got all dressed up to go out on a date with the guy she married, Kevin I think his name was, and the outfit she had on . . . well, the colors, you know, they just didn't go with her blond hair. I shouldn't've said anything, but I did and she got real mad, I mean *real* mad, and started yelling four-letter words at me. I tried to tell her I was sorry, but she wouldn't listen, just started after me like, you know, like she wanted to break my neck or something. I ran into the bathroom and locked the door. She pounded on it a few times and I guess after that she calmed down and went out. Well, I was so shook up I stayed in the bathroom for a good half hour, until I was sure she was gone."

"What happened when you saw her again?"

"Well, she acted like nothing had happened. I told her she'd scared me pretty bad and she said, 'Well, don't ever criticize my clothes again,' and I said I wouldn't and that was the end of it."

"And that was the only incident?" Runyon asked.

"The only one. Francine was real sweet most of the time, you know?"

Charlene Kepler, out.

Now he had nothing to tell Bryn.

10

BRYN DARBY

She stood looking at her reflection in the bathroom mirror, fingering the vial of Xanax and wondering how many of the little white pills it would take to put her out of her misery.

A dozen or so would probably do it. This was a new prescription, the vial almost full—more than enough. Wash them down with a couple of glasses of wine, throw in four or five Vicodin to make sure, and when she started feeling the effects lie down in bed with the lights on to wait for the dark. Easy, painless. Just go to sleep and no more hurt or fear or black depression, no more looking at what she was looking at right now.

The face in the mirror was like one of those split theatrical masks, only hers wasn't half tragedy and half comedy; it was half living and half dead. That was how she thought of the left side, not as paralyzed or frozen, the euphemisms used by the doctors and everybody else, but as dead. Part of her already dead. Pale waxy flesh, the corner of the mouth puckered so that she couldn't open it all the way, couldn't eat or drink in a normal fashion, dribbled and drooled like a baby. Puckered lines around the eye, too, and the optic nerve damaged so that she had cloudy vision out of it. The muscles and nerves already atrophying, no way to stop it, no chance of recovery. Most of the time she had no feeling on that side, but sometimes, and now was one of them, there was a faint burning sensation as if she were standing too close to a stove or heater. Her doctor claimed that this was psychosomatic, a phantom sensation, because of the extent of the nerve damage. Dead tissue has no feeling. Death has no feeling. Except that it did. The dead side of her face *burned*.

How many times had she stood here like this, thinking these same thoughts? More than she could count after the stroke and before she met Jake. Only a couple since he'd come into her life, the one good thing that had made living bearable the past few months. Somebody she could lean on, take strength from; somebody to drive away the loneliness and despair for short periods; somebody she cared about beside Bobby, at a time when she believed she would never care about anyone else again. If it hadn't been for Jake and Bobby, she would have mixed the Xanax and Vicodin and wine cocktail by now. And the rest of her would be as dead as the left side of her face.

The depression was bad tonight, as bleak and overpowering as it had ever been. Worrying about that bitch Francine hurting Bobby again, *really* hurting him, putting him in the hospital, putting him in a coffin . . . it was maddening because there was nothing Bryn could do short of giving in to her impulses and destroying the woman. Running away with Bobby to some place where he'd be safe wasn't an option. She didn't have enough money to travel very far or hide for very long; wherever she and Bobby went, Robert had the money and the resources to find them. And then he'd make sure she never saw her son again.

Jake was doing everything he could—he'd already found out that Francine had a probable history of abuse with her two sisters—but it wasn't enough. The sister in Berkeley had mental problems and wouldn't talk about the abuse; the sister in Ojai wouldn't, either. How could they expose Francine for what she was before she hurt Bobby so badly that his father could no longer deny the truth? All Robert could or wanted to see now was that falsely sweet young face.

Still, Jake was the only hope she had. Keep the faith in him, pray for Bobby's safety . . . otherwise, the despair would consume her. And then she really would mix and swallow that last cocktail.

Bryn put the Xanax back into the medicine cabinet, turned away from the mirror. Her hands and face were sweaty; she dried them on a towel, then retied the scarf over the dead half. Even when she was alone in the house, she'd taken to hiding it behind cloth. Out of sight, out of mind—that was the idea, anyway, even if it didn't always work.

In the kitchen she poured another glass of wine. How many did this make today? She'd lost count. But it would have to be the last. She had to walk a fine line with alcohol. Just enough took the edge off her anxiety, allowed her to continue functioning; too much made the depression worse.

She lifted the glass, then set it down again. She really didn't need another drink—she'd had too much already. The last glass was what had led her into the bathroom, to remove the scarf and stand there wallowing in her misery. Already there was a dull ache in her temples and her mouth was dry and sour tasting; any more alcohol and she'd suffer for it in the morning.

She took a small funnel out of the utility drawer, poured the wine back into the bottle, and returned the bottle to the fridge. The house held an empty kind of silence, broken only by an occasional settling creak and the humming and rattling of the wind outside. She'd had a CD of Gilbert and Sullivan's *Pirates of Penzance* playing earlier, ~~spritely~~ music in an effort to ward off the demons, but it had run through and stopped. She thought about starting it again, decided she was no longer in the mood for comic opera. Another CD? Something on television? They didn't appeal, either.

sprightly

What she really wanted was to talk to Bobby, make sure he was all right. But she'd called last night and Robert had grudgingly let her talk to him and he seemed okay then, if still quiet and distant. She couldn't keep calling every night. Robert would refuse to put the boy on, harangue her about bothering him at home, and then hang up; he'd done that before. And if she called and he wasn't home and Francine answered, the bitch would hang up right away. That had happened before, too.

Would Robert let her know immediately if anything serious happened to Bobby? He might, and he might not. She might not know about it for hours, even days. . . .

"Stop," she said aloud. "Stop, stop."

She went down the hall into her office, booted up her Mac, and opened the Hardiman file. Her current project—designing an extensive new Web site for Hardiman Industries. It was half-finished, the graphics satisfactory so far, but she hadn't been able to work steadily on it for days. The deadline was looming; she'd have to get back to it soon or risk losing the commission. Now? Not now. Her thoughts were muzzy and the color images blurred as she stared at the screen. Tomorrow morning . . .

And the rest of tonight?

It was too early for bed. Maybe she could do a little more work on one of the three unfinished watercolor paintings. . . . Bad idea, for the same reason she couldn't concentrate on the Hardiman Web site design. Her headache had worsened; she felt a little sick to her stomach.

Warm bath, she thought, that might help. In the bathroom again she drank a glass of Alka-Seltzer to relieve the queasy feeling. She was leaning into the tub to turn on the water taps when the doorbell rang.

Jake? He usually called before he came over . . . unless he had something new and important to tell her. She hurried out to the front door, unlocked it, and pulled it open without first looking through the peephole. And sucked in her breath and felt her body go rigid because it wasn't Jake standing there in the glow of the porch light.

"Hello, Bryn," Francine Whalen said through one of her bright, empty smiles.

". . . What do you want here?"

"It's about Bobby. Can I come in? I won't stay long."

"What about Bobby? Where is he?"

"Home with his father."

"Is he all right?"

"Of course he's all right. Well? Are you going to let me in?"

Reluctantly Bryn complied. Once Francine was inside with the door closed, the smile disappeared. She had a longish, narrow face framed by long, feathery blond hair—an expensive designer cut to go with the expensive leather jacket and tight slacks and Gucci boots she wore. All paid for by Robert, no doubt. Her eyes were her most striking feature, large gray eyes with irises so pale they were almost translucent. The kind that men would find warm and smoky, that to Bryn gave the exact opposite effect. Ice eyes.

"The reason I'm here," the woman said, "is to tell you straight to your face—stop trying to turn Bobby against me."

"What're you talking about?"

"Filling his head with nonsense, trying to convince him that I'm some sort of wicked witch."

"That's just what you are."

"Oh? So now you admit that's what you've been doing."

"You're the one who turned him against you, not me. And we both know the reason."

"Yes? What reason?"

"You've been hitting him, hurting him. A little boy, for God's sake."

"That's a damn lie," Francine said. But nothing changed in her expression; no shock or surprise or outrage. The face of unrepentant guilt. "Why would I do something like that?"

"Yes, exactly. Why? Why did you fracture his arm? Why do you leave bruises all over his body?"

"I did no such things. He gets into fights with other boys his age and he's accident-prone."

"Like hell. You, you're the one."

"Did Bobby tell you I was hurting him?"

Bryn didn't answer. Rage was like a probe moving through her; the dead side of her face burned as if it were on fire. She locked her fingers together at her waist to keep them still, keep herself under control.

"Well? Did he?"

"He didn't have to."

"I'll bet he's never said a bad word about me."

"He hates you. He said that much."

"Natural in a boy his age to have some hostile feelings toward the woman who replaces his mother in his father's affection. Particularly when the mother reinforces it, stuffs his head with lies."

"I've never lied to my son and I never will."

"Bullshit." The word sounded twice as ugly coming out of that angelic mouth. "You've done your damnedest to poison my relationship with Bobby. You'd better stop, Bryn, I'm warning you. I won't stand for any more of it and neither will Robert."

"And I'm warning you—hurt him again and you'll be sorry."

"Oh, really? And how are you going to make me sorry?"

"I'll find a way."

"No, you won't. You're as helpless as a baby. Not to mention paranoid and delusional—the stroke crippled your mind as well as your face. Robert says so; that's why he left you. I say so, too."

"And you're a cold, sadistic cunt."

"Call me any names you like to my face, but don't put them in Bobby's head anymore. If you do, Robert and I will see to it that you don't have any more time with him." The smile flashed on again, tight-lipped and humorless. "We can do that—Robert can—and I promise you, we will."

An image flared up behind Bryn's eyes: herself leaping forward, hands unclenching and hooking into claws that ripped furrows down the sides of that smug, smirking face. She struggled against the urge, fought it down. Felt herself shaking visibly now. The hot taste of bile filled her throat; the question she managed to push through it had a liquidy sound.

"Did Robert send you to tell me that?"

"No. He doesn't know I'm here and I'll deny it if you tell him. This is between you and me, Bryn. Robert's mine now and so is Bobby. I took them away from you and I'm going to keep them and you'd better resign yourself to the fact and quit trying to cause trouble for us. Do you understand what I'm saying?"

Bryn's throat muscles worked, but she couldn't get any more words out.

"I think you do. Good," Francine said. And what she did then was so shocking Bryn was incapable of any reaction: she reached out, almost casually, and yanked the scarf off and dropped it fluttering to the floor. "I've always wanted to see what that side of your face looks like. My God, you're even uglier than I thought. No wonder Robert couldn't stand the sight of you."

Francine opened the door, turned long enough to smile her poison-sweet smile again, and then vanished into the darkness.

11

I'd been at the agency just long enough on Thursday morning to pour a cup of coffee from the pot on the anteroom hot plate when Tamara came out of her office. "The call that just came in on line one," she said, "I think you'd better pick up."

"Who is it?"

"Judith LoPresti. David Virden's fiancée."

"What does she want?"

"She'll tell you. I'll listen in."

I carried the coffee into my office. We still hadn't heard from Virden and I figured he was nursing his grudge and wanted nothing more to do with us. But he hadn't put stop payments on the two checks he'd written to the agency; Tamara had contacted the bank yesterday afternoon, late, and both of them had gone through.

Judith LoPresti had a low, well-rounded voice—an intelligent voice. It was also a worried voice, with an undertone of scare in it. "Have you seen or heard from David since Tuesday?"

"No, we haven't. He was here about one o'clock to pick up our report and the Church papers."

"Yes, I know about that. The last time I talked to him, he told me you'd found Roxanne McManus."

"Well, there seems to be some question about that," I said.

"Question?"

Tamara was still on the line. She said, "He called me later that afternoon, Ms. LoPresti, upset because he said the woman we located wasn't his ex-wife."

". . . I don't understand."

"Neither do we. Everything we found out says that she is."

I said, "I left a couple of messages for him later that day, but he hasn't returned the calls."

"He's missing," Judith LoPresti said.

"Missing?"

"Since sometime Tuesday. He didn't show up to meet me that evening as we'd arranged. He hasn't been to his office—he missed an important conference yesterday. He hasn't been home, either. I went to his apartment last night—the mail and newspapers hadn't been picked up." The scare in her voice had become a little more pronounced. "It's not like him to just go off somewhere without a word to me or anyone else. Frankly, I'm afraid something may have happened to him."

"Did you check the local hospitals?"

"Every one in the city, on the Peninsula, here in the South Bay. He wasn't in an accident or anything like that."

Not necessarily true, but I kept the thought to myself. "What kind of car does he drive?"

"A black Porsche Cayman. I bought it for him for his birthday."

Some birthday present. More to the point, brand-new Porsches can be targets for carjackers and their drivers targets for violent muggers. Dogpatch's crime rate wasn't the worst in the city by any stretch, but there were other neighborhoods not far away that had more than their share of gangs and street thugs who didn't always confine commission of felonies to their own turf.

"Would you happen to know the license number?"

"As a matter of fact I would. It's a vanity plate— VRDNEXEC."

Short for "Virden Executive." The man thought a lot of himself, all right.

"Is the Porsche the only vehicle he owns?"

"Yes."

"Have you been to the police, Ms. LoPresti?"

"Last night, after I left David's apartment. But they said I'd have to wait until today to file a missing-person report . . . something about a mandatory seventy-two-hour waiting period. The officer I spoke to wasn't very helpful; he seemed to think I was overreacting. I wasn't and I'm not. If David was all right, he'd have contacted me by now."

"Since this is the last place he was seen, you might want to file a report with the San Francisco police."

"They must get dozens of missing-person reports. Will they do something right away to find David? I don't believe they will."

I let that pass without comment. She was closer to being right than wrong.

She said then, "Is there anything you can do?"

"Well . . ."

Tamara said, "We can try, if you'd like to hire us."

"Yes." Immediate answer; Ms. LoPresti had already made that decision. "Yes, I would."

"We'll need your signature on a contract, and a retainer check."

"I can leave now and be in the city in an hour and a half."

"Be expecting you."

End of conversation, without another word from me. So be it. Tamara was in charge now, and she'd never been bashful when it came to drumming up business. I don't necessarily approve of the kind of direct approach she'd used on Judith LoPresti, but then the agency wasn't half as successful when I was running it on solo power and antiquated methods. Once, years back, Tamara had called me a dinosaur. Right. Edging up on extinction like the rest of those lumbering creatures.

She came into my office as I was taking a swig of some of the now lukewarm coffee. "R. L. McManus," she said.

"What about her?"

"Turns out not to be Virden's wife and now Virden's gone missing. Pretty funny coincidence."

"Hold on," I said. "He called you after he left Canine Customers."

"He could've gone back."

"Why would he do that?"

"Try to find out who the woman really is."

"And then what? You think she did something to him?"

"Criminals don't want to get caught, right?"

"If she's a criminal," I said. "And even if she is, it's a big jump from thief to murderer."

"Not if they're backed into a corner."

"Any number of other things could've happened to Virden. Mugging, carjacking. Even a planned disappearance."

"With all that LoPresti green waiting for him? And after

all the trouble he went to to track down his ex-wives and get them to sign annulment papers?"

"All right. Point taken."

"McManus was the last person he saw before he dropped off the radar."

"That we know about."

"I say we keep investigating her."

"Agreed. But check on the other possibilities first; see if anything turns up on Virden or that Porsche of his."

Nothing did. Virden's name didn't appear on any Bay Area police blotter, either as victim or complainant, and there was no record of a black Porsche Cayman with a VRDNEXEC license plate having been in an accident or found abandoned or towed and impounded in S.F. or any of the Peninsula cities.

Tamara said when she was done running her checks, "Right back to McManus. Want me to talk to her, see what she has to say?"

"No, I'll do it."

"When?"

I sighed, though not audibly enough for Tamara to hear. "As soon as we have the face-to-face with our new client."

Judith LoPresti was true to her time estimate: she walked into the agency almost exactly an hour and a half later. Attractive woman; Virden's interest in marrying her wasn't strictly monetary. Thirty or so, long red hair, green eyes, a model's slender figure. Regal bearing, too, enhanced by the expensively tailored off-white suit she wore. Around her neck on a chain was a small gold cross, testimony to her faith. Very calm and matter-of-fact—you had to look closely to see the worry lines and missed-sleep smudges beneath artfully applied makeup.

We got the financial end out of the way first. Tamara had the standard agency contract ready; Ms. LoPresti gave it a hurried read-through, saying, "David was satisfied with it, I'm sure it's fine," signed it, and wrote a check to cover the retainer. Then we interviewed her in my office.

She had questions of her own first. "On the phone you said David called you Tuesday afternoon, upset because the woman you found isn't Roxanne McManus."

"That's what he said, yes."

"How is that possible?"

"We're not sure yet. It's one of the things we'll be looking into."

Tamara said, "But we didn't make a mistake. I double-checked our research—it's accurate."

"I believe you. We researched detective agencies before we chose yours. You come highly recommended."

Vindicated, Tamara smiled and nodded. I wondered if she'd noticed Judith LoPresti's use of the plural pronoun, indicating Virden wasn't as much the alpha party in their relationship as he'd let on. Probably she had. She's smarter than I am and she doesn't miss much.

"The report you gave David—I'd like a copy of it."

"I've already printed one out. I'll get it for you when we're done here."

Ms. LoPresti said, "David would certainly know a woman he was married to, even after eight years. She couldn't have changed that much."

"Not likely."

"Well, then? Is this woman an impostor?"

"It's one possibility," I said. Better to be noncommittal at this point.

"Could she have had anything to do with David's disappearance?"

"He'd already left her home when he called here."

"But he could have gone back."

"Yes, he could have."

"Did he tell you where he was calling from?"

"No. It might've been his car—faint background noises."

"Then why didn't he call me with the news? My cell was on the entire day."

I kept quiet. So did Tamara. She knew better than to share her dire speculations with a client.

Routine questions, then, me asking most of them by tacit agreement.

"I take it your fiancé has never done anything like this before? Willfully disappeared for a short period without telling anyone?"

"Not in the year I've known him. Never, I'm sure. He's simply not that sort of person."

"Business problems of any kind that you know about?"

"No. He has a very secure position with Hungerford and Son."

"Personal problems? Enemies?"

"None. Everyone likes David."

I didn't and Tamara didn't and he'd been divorced three times, so the answer was ingenuous. So was her response to my next question.

"Pardon me for asking this, but we need to know. Does he have a history of mental problems or alcohol or chemical abuse?"

"Absolutely not. David is the most stable and sober man I've ever known." The implication from her tone being that she wouldn't have accepted his marriage proposal if he was anything but.

"Does he have any friends in the city, anyone he might contact if he had a problem or an emergency?"

"No. The only people he knows here are casual business acquaintances. We've driven up a few times for dinner, the symphony, a show. He would have introduced me to any friends he had here, or at least told me about them."

Not necessarily, but I let it go. "Is there anywhere you can think of that he might have gone voluntarily?"

"No. And certainly not without notifying me or his office."

"Do you own a second home?"

"My family has a house at Lake Tahoe, but David would never go there by himself. Besides, it's closed up this time of year."

"Okay. One more thing. A photo, if you have one."

"Yes, but it's wallet size."

"That'll do."

It was a nicely framed head-and-shoulders snapshot, Virden smiling all over his handsome face, one eye half-closed as though he'd been snapped in the middle of a wink. She seemed reluctant to part with it. "It's my favorite," she said, "and I'm not sure I still have the negative. I'd like it back when you find David."

"Of course."

"You'll start looking for him right away?"

I said we would, and that we'd let her know as soon as we found out anything she should know.

"Thank you. I hope . . ." She stopped, nibbled her lower lip, and substituted a wan smile for what she'd been about to say. Scared, all right, and trying not to show it. Her bearing remained regal, the wan smile fixed, as I showed her out.

When I came back, Tamara said, "No nonsense and a lot of cool. I like her and I feel sorry for her."

"Same here."

"Just the opposite of Virden. I wonder what she sees in him."

"Something you and I don't, evidently."

"Gonna get hurt, whether we find him or not. Women ought to have better sense than to fall in love with guys like him."

"Love doesn't work that way, kiddo."

"Not telling me anything I don't know. Look at my track record with men."

"You'll meet the right one someday. And you'll know it when you do."

"Uh-huh," she said. "So how come every wrong dude I ever hooked up with seemed like Mr. Right at the time?"

12

The *Room for Rent* sign was absent from the fence in front of the McManus house. No surprise there; it didn't take long to find single tenants with modest needs in neighborhoods like Dogpatch that had easy public-transit access to downtown. The driveway was empty today, but the house wasn't.

Déjà vu when I thumbed the doorbell: the Hound of the Baskervilles started his furious barking, a woman's commanding voice said, "Quiet, Thor!" to shut him up, and Jane Carson opened up wearing her toothy smile. One good look at me and the smile turned upside down.

"Oh," she said, "it's you again."

"Me again. I'd like to speak to Ms. McManus."

"She's not home."

"When do you expect her back?"

"No specific time. She has a busy schedule."

"Me, too. Busy, busy."

As before, the dog sat on his haunches behind and to one side of the woman, watching me with his yellow eyes. Maybe he sensed her chilly attitude or maybe he just didn't like me any more than I liked him; the eyes looked hot and his fangs were visible in what I took to be a silent growl.

"What did you wish to see R.L. about?"

I held up Virden's photo. Carson looked at it, but only for a couple of seconds. "This man."

"I've never seen him before. Who is he?"

"David Virden, Ms. McManus's ex-husband. The man who came to see her Tuesday afternoon."

"I don't know anything about that. I was away Tuesday afternoon."

"And she didn't mention his visit?"

"No, she didn't."

"Say anything about him after I was here on Monday?"

"No."

"Tell me, Ms. Carson, just what is it you do here? Employee, tenant, companion?"

"I don't see where that's any of your business."

"Simple question."

"All right, then, I'll give you a simple answer. I work with the dogs."

"Been with Canine Customers long?"

"Not long, no." Very cold and crisp now. Thor's ears pricked up; a little more of his fangs showed. "Is there anything else?"

I got out one of my business cards, jotted a "please contact me ASAP" note on the back, and handed it to Carson—doing it all slowly with one eye on Thor. He sat still, but the yellow eyes followed every move I made. "Make sure she gets this, please. I'll expect to—"

That was as far as I got, because she shut the door in my face.

. . .

I made a fifteen-minute driving canvass over a radius of several blocks. There was no sign of Virden's black Porsche Cayman—or any other model or color Porsche. Finding him or his vehicle wasn't going to be that easy.

McManus's immediate neighbors were the next order of business. I didn't make any effort to conceal my continued presence in the area; in fact, I parked across the street from Canine Customers and took my time walking around. If Carson was paying attention, I wanted her to see me and relay the information to McManus. It wouldn't bother them much if they had nothing to hide. On the other hand, it might shake them up to know they were being investigated. Shake up people with something to hide and it can lead to mistakes and answers.

House canvassing is not one of my favorite tasks. Most city residents are leery of strangers these days, no matter how well dressed, polite, and nonthreatening, and if I have to flash my ID, it turns some hostile and makes others close up like cactus flowers at sundown. These were the reactions I got from the first five neighbors who were home and took the trouble to answer their doorbells. Only two deigned to look at Virden's photo and none of the five could or would own up to seeing him or his Porsche in the neighborhood on Tuesday afternoon.

The sixth person I talked to, a woman in one of the houses on Minnesota Street catercorner to the McManus place, was the only one who had anything to tell me—of a sort. And not without some initial confusion and difficulty.

She was in her late sixties, the owner of a pile of frizzy gray hair, a pair of beadily alert gray eyes, plump cheeks red stained with broken capillaries, and a set of false teeth that had been improperly fitted and gave her something of an overbite. She took one look at me and said in disgusted tones, "Oh, God, a new one."

"No, ma'am, I'm not selling—"

"You're pretty old, aren't you?"

"Old?"

"To be chasing after young women. Laurie's not even forty yet."

"I'm afraid you have me—"

"Have you? Not me, mister. You or any other man, now that my husband's gone to his reward." She spoke with a slight lisp, the false teeth clicking now and then like little finger snaps. "My daughter's got no morals, same like her father. Not much taste, either, I must say. You're old enough to *be* her father . . . and married, too."

"I am, yes, but—"

"Not even trying to hide it, wedding ring right there on your finger. You ought to be ashamed of yourself."

"You don't understand—"

"The devil I don't understand. I know all about men like you, I was married to a cheating old goat myself for thirty-seven years. Go away; go back to your wife. Laurie's not here."

She started to close the door. I got a foot in the way, the photograph up between her face and mine, and said fast so she couldn't interrupt, "I don't know any woman named Laurie. I'm looking for a missing person, the man in this photo, he was in this neighborhood on Tuesday afternoon."

She batted her eyes, clicked her teeth, flushed a little, and said, "Oh my God," in a subdued and mortified tone. "I thought you were screwing my daughter."

"So I gathered."

"I'm sorry. You must think I'm awful, talking to you the way I did. . . ."

"No, ma'am," I lied. I eased the photo a little closer. "Do you recognize this man?"

She squinted, clicked, and lisped, "No. Never saw anybody looks like that."

"He was driving a new black Porsche."

"I don't know anything about cars. I wouldn't know a Porsche from a petunia."

"Sports car. Pretty distinctive."

"Never saw it. The man's missing, you say? He live around here?"

"No. Visiting R. L. McManus."

"Oh, the dog woman. New boarder over there?"

"No. He was there on a personal matter."

"Gate sign's down, so she's got a new one. That's why I asked. Steady string in and out of there, you'd think some of them would stay longer than they do. Must be the damn dogs barking all the time that drives them away."

"How well do you know her, Mrs.—?"

"Hightower, Selma Hightower. Just to talk to, that's all. Standoffish. Keeps to herself."

"Jane Carson?"

"Hah. No, and I keep my distance when I see her."

"Why is that?"

"Always has that big black dog with her. Dogs like that make me nervous. Supposed to be well trained, but the way they look at you . . ." She shivered, double-clicked. "Brrrr."

"Can you tell me what their relationship is?"

"Whose relationship? Her and that dog?"

"The two women. Does Ms. Carson, who works for Ms. McManus, live on the premises?"

"Lives there. Moved in together six or seven years ago. What they do is none of my business." A valid enough comment, which she spoiled by adding, "Couple of lesbians, if you ask me. Hardly ever see a man around the place, except when one shows up with a dog to be boarded."

"All the boarders are ladies, then?"

"How should I know? You think I go peeking under their tails?"

I said, as patiently as I could, "I meant the people who rent a room there."

"Oh. Well, why didn't you say so? Almost all women, that's right. One old man early last year, must've been eighty—he's the only one I remember."

"One room for rent or more than one?"

"Just one. That's what Rose told me."

"Rose?"

"She lived over there for a few months a while back. Nice person, my age, widow like me only she didn't have any kids, lucky her. We had a lot in common. Bingo, *All My Children,* a toddy now and then. She liked her toddies, Rose did. That's how she met the dog woman. Not McManus, the other one. Carson."

". . . I'm not sure I understand what you mean."

She gave me a well-then-you-must-be-dense look. "In a cocktail lounge. Both of them having toddies and they got to talking and that's how Rose ended up here. She couldn't afford the rents down there anymore."

"Down where?"

"What they call SoMa now. That's where Rose and the dog woman were having their toddies."

"Do you remember the name of the cocktail lounge?"

"Rose never said. Why do you care what cocktail lounge?"

"Curiosity. What was Rose's last name?"

"O'Day. Rose O'Day. Pretty name."

"Yes. When did—"

"Irish," Mrs. Hightower said.

". . . Pardon?"

"Rose. She was Irish."

"When did she move out?"

"Well, let's see. Must've been more than three years now. That's right, three years in February." Click, frown, double-click. "Kind of funny," she said.

"How so?"

"Never said good-bye. Just up and left. And us with a date to play bingo over at the church. I saw the dog woman, McManus, down at the market a few days afterward and asked her how come Rose left so sudden. Said she went back to Michigan— that's where she's from, Saginaw, Michigan, like in the song. Moved back to Saginaw, Michigan, to live with her brother."

"I see."

"No, you don't," Selma Hightower said, "and neither do I. Rose told me she was an only child."

"Well, people sometimes say that if they're estranged from a relative—"

"Hah. Rose didn't have anybody to be estranged *from*. She didn't have anybody, period. Alone in the world after her husband went to his reward. All her family dead and gone and her all alone in the world."

. . .

Half an hour after I left Mrs. Hightower, I finally located somebody who'd seen David Virden on Tuesday. Two somebodies, in fact. Both of them in the same place—a watering hole on Third just around the corner from 20th Street called, appropriately if unappealingly, The Dog Hole.

It was one of those venerable neighborhood places that cater to a mixed clientele. At its peak hours you'd probably find blue-collar workers, Yuppies, bikers, scroungers, retired people, lonely individuals of both sexes looking for companionship of one kind or another, and maybe an upscale hooker or two trolling for customers. At this time of day, early afternoon, what you had was a small core of habitual drinkers and pensioners with no better spot to spend their time. Three men were drinking beer and playing cribbage in one of a row of high-backed booths. A rail-thin man in his seventies and a heavily rouged fat woman twenty years younger occupied stools at the bar, neither of them having anything to do with the other.

The bartender was a bulky guy in his forties—a weight lifter, judging from the bulge of his pecs and biceps in a tight short-sleeved shirt. I ordered a draft Anchor Steam, and when he brought it I showed him Virden's photograph and asked my question. He gave the snapshot a bored study, started to shake his head, looked again, and said, "Yeah, he was in here. Double shot of Jameson, beer back."

"What time?"

"Around this time."

"Alone?" I asked.

"All alone. You a cop?"

"Private. He's missing; I'm looking for him."

"That right?" But not as if he cared. Life outside a gym and a weight room probably bored him silly. "Never saw him before or since."

The old gent got off his stool and sidled down to where I was, bringing his empty glass with him. "Mind if I have a look?" I held the photo up so he could squint at it through rimless glasses. "Yep, I seen him, too. Stranger dressed real nice, suit and tie. But it wasn't around this time."

"No? When was it?"

"Well . . ." He set his empty on the bar and licked his lips in a mildly suggestive way. I gestured to the bartender, who shrugged and filled the glass from a bottle of port wine.

"Thank you, sir. To your health." He had some of his port, an almost dainty sip as if he intended to make it last. "Must've been about one thirty when the fella come in. No more'n five minutes after I did. Remember, Stan?"

Another shrug. "If you say so."

"You didn't happen to talk to him?" I asked.

"No, sir. He wasn't the sociable type."

"Why do you say that?"

"Fella had a mad-on about something. Face like a thundercloud, you know what I mean? Sat there and swallowed his drinks and then all of a sudden he smacks the bar and out he goes."

"Smacked the bar?"

"Real hard. Went out of here like something just bit him on his ass."

Or he'd made up his mind about something, I thought. Like maybe going back for another conversation with the woman who was supposed to be his ex-wife.

. . .

I was out of The Dog Hole and in my car, but not driving yet, when my cell phone went off. Small favors. Or so I thought until I answered the call.

"R. L. McManus. Why are you harassing me?" This in a clipped voice as cold as ice.

"I'd hardly call two brief visits to your home harassment, Ms. McManus."

"I told you on Monday I wanted nothing more to do with you or my ex-husband. And I told him the same thing when he showed up here the next day."

"Did you, now."

"In no uncertain terms. And I suppose he sent you back to bother me with more of his annulment nonsense?"

"No. As a matter of fact, I haven't spoken to him since Monday."

"Then why were you at my home again today?"

"Because he's gone missing."

One, two, three seconds before she said, "Missing?"

"No one's seen him since Tuesday afternoon."

"Well, I don't know anything about that. He was here for no more than five minutes and I haven't seen or heard from him since."

"Must've been kind of an awkward meeting."

"It was. Awkward and unnecessary."

"How did he look to you?"

". . . What kind of question is that?"

"Eight years since your divorce. Had he changed much?"

"Not very much, no."

"Recognized him immediately, then."

"I'm not likely to forget a man I was married to, am I?"

"And he recognized you right away."

"Of course he did. I haven't changed that much, either." Suspicion in her voice now. "What are you getting at?"

"All you talked about is the annulment, is that right?"

"Yes, that's right, and that's the last question I'm going to answer. If you don't leave me alone, I'll sue you for harassment. You can tell David that goes for him, too, when you find him. Is that understood?"

What's understood, lady, I thought, is that you're a damn liar. But I didn't say it. I didn't say anything, just pressed the Off button on the cell.

I was pretty near convinced that Tamara was right about McManus. People who overreact by threatening lawsuits usually have plenty to hide. Question was, just how dirty was she?

13

JAKE RUNYON

Another busy road day. Over to Oakland, first thing, for a deposition in an insurance fraud investigation. Then down to Union City for another interview with the second witness in the hit-and-run accident case: the attorney for the injured party had some questions he wanted answered to verify the man's reliability. Then back across the bay on the Dumbarton Bridge and up to Palo Alto to talk to a woman who had new information on the subject of a backburnered skip-trace.

Ordinarily Runyon didn't mind that kind of workday. Preferred it, in fact. When he'd first joined the agency, he'd asked for assignments that kept him on the move and put in as much weekend work as he could without requesting overtime pay. And most of his spare time had been spent behind the wheel; long drives that he'd pretended were to familiarize himself with the highways and back roads of the greater Bay Area but in reality were excuses to keep him moving, keep his mind occupied and focused on externals. That was how he got through his waking hours. Once he'd accepted the fact that his and Joshua's estrangement was permanent, work became his only reason for existing. When he wasn't on a job, he shunned company. Had no use for casual friends, didn't want another woman even for a single night because he'd lost, or believed then that he'd lost, his sex drive.

But he hadn't thought of himself as a lonely man. Empty, consumed by loss—a loner by choice and circumstance. It wasn't until he met Bryn that he realized the truth about himself. And was finally able to let go of his grief, drag himself out of his self-imposed limbo.

Bryn and her son and Francine Whalen were the reason the long road day dragged by. Frustration nagged at him. He kept trying to devise some way to expose Whalen for what she was, but without support from the people she'd wounded he was hamstrung. An outsider, already walking a tightrope line. Confronting her directly, trying to intimidate her, was sure to backfire. You could intimidate a rational person whose emotions were under control, but not a calculating, unstable, and possibly sadistic one. It might even trigger her violent impulses, with Bobby as the handiest target.

Francine, out.

Another face-up with Robert Darby wouldn't get him anywhere, either. Just be another exercise in futility. The man was too deep in love and denial to listen to reason until the truth was shoved in his face. And then it might be too late.

Darby, out.

What did that leave him? Not much. Another go at Bobby, if he could manage it. The boy had opened up to him a little on Saturday; maybe there was a way to gain enough of his trust to counteract Francine's hold on him. Talk again to Gwen Whalen, Tracy Holland, the ex-husband, try to convince at least one of them to come forward. See if he could track down the man Francine had lived with before moving in with Charlene Kepler, David or Darren something.

But the first person he wanted to see tonight was Bryn.

He drove back into the city on 280. It was a couple of minutes shy of four o'clock and he was on Nineteenth Avenue, waiting at one of the stoplights fronting the S.F. State campus, when his cell phone vibrated.

He checked the screen. Bryn. He clicked on, saying, "I was just thinking about you—"

"Jake," she said, and he knew instantly that something was wrong. Her voice had a clotted sound, as if her throat was full of phlegm. When she spoke again, he could hear the kind of ragged breathing that comes with near hysteria. "Jake, I need you . . . I don't know what to do. . . ."

"What is it? What's happened?"

"Can't, I can't . . . not on the phone. Can you come here . . . now, right away?"

"Where are you? Home?"

"No. Robert's flat in the Marina."

Jesus. "Is Bobby all right?"

"Yes . . . yes. Hurry, Jake. Please hurry."

"On my way. Twenty minutes."

Heavy traffic on Nineteenth Avenue made it twenty-five minutes. Runyon didn't let himself think on the way. You got an emergency call, you waited until you arrived at the scene and assessed the situation before you opened up your mind.

Avila was a short, slanting street off busy Marina Boulevard, Robert Darby's address within shouting distance of the Marina Green and the city's West Harbor yacht clubs beyond. Runyon parked illegally at the corner, the hell with it, and ran to the brown stucco building mid-block and leaned on Darby's bell in the tiny foyer. The answering buzz came almost immediately. Inside, up a flight of carpeted stairs. Bryn was waiting for him in an open doorway at the top.

She'd composed herself in the time it had taken him to get there, evident in the way she stood with her back straight and her arms down at her sides. But it was a brittle kind of calm; the aftereffects of shock and near panic showed in her eyes, in the paleness of the undamaged side of her face. But what caught his attention first, before any of that, was the drying smear of blood across the front of her blouse.

"Are you hurt?"

"No."

"The blood—Bobby's?"

Bryn shook her head, but Runyon couldn't tell if it was a negative or reflex.

"Where is he?"

"In his bedroom. I washed the blood off his face, made him lie down with an ice pack . . ."

"You said he was all right."

"He is now. She hit him in the face, there was blood all over him when I got here. From his nose, from a ring cut on his cheek. His nose isn't broken, thank God."

"Francine. Where is she?"

"The kitchen. She . . . oh, God, Jake . . ."

Bryn turned away from him, walked to the middle of the room. Steadily, if rigidly, her arms still hanging down and pressed close to her body. Runyon eased the door shut, went to stand close in front of her. Peripherally he was aware that the living room had too much furniture, that the décor was done in a confused jumble of colors—blue, green, orange, brown. But the only color he had eyes for was the crimson on her blouse.

"You'd better sit down," he said.

"No. I can't sit still."

"Where's the kitchen?"

"I don't want to go in there again."

"You don't have to. Just point me to it."

"Through the swing door over there."

He left her, pushed through the swing door. The kitchen, big, lit by track lighting between a pair of skylights, was at an angle beyond a formal dining room. One step into it, he pulled up short.

Bad, all right. As bad as it gets.

Francine Whalen lay on the floor between an island stove and a dinette table, twisted onto her back with her skirt hiked up over her thighs, eyes open with that milk-glass cloudiness he'd seen too many times before. Blood all over her blouse, too, and on the floor around her. The knife in her chest had a curved bone handle stained with bloody fingermarks. The lingering aroma of something she'd been baking contrasted sickeningly with the carnage.

Runyon backed up, turned, returned to the living room. Bryn was pacing in slow, restless steps; she stopped and stood still again when she saw him. A little color had come back into the right side of her face. The paisley scarf over the crippled side hung askew; he rearranged it so the stroke-frozen flesh was completely covered. She didn't move or speak until he finished.

"I did it," she said then. "I didn't mean to, but I killed Francine."

What happened, Bryn?"

"She showed up at my home last night, threatened me in a cold-blooded, vicious way . . . I was afraid she might do something else to Bobby just to spite me. I shouldn't have come here today, I know that, but I couldn't help it, I had to make sure he was all right." Flat voice, without inflection, but Runyon could hear the undercurrent of emotions like a distant sea whisper. "She didn't want to let me in. I knew something was wrong by the way she acted. I pushed past her, and when I saw Bobby, all the blood, what she'd just done to him, I . . . went a little crazy. I screamed at her and she screamed back. Then she tried to claw my face. I slapped her, she slapped me and ran into the kitchen, I ran after her. What happened after that . . . it's not very clear. We were struggling and the next thing I knew she had that knife in her hand. I grabbed her arm, twisted it, tried to make her drop the knife, but instead she . . . somehow it got between us and . . . the next thing I knew I was standing over her with blood on my hands."

Her hands were clean now. She saw Runyon looking at them, at the fresh-looking Band-Aid on one finger, and said, "I washed it off in the bathroom. Some of it was mine . . . she must have cut my finger in the struggle."

"Did Bobby see it happen?"

"No. God, no. He never came out of his bedroom."

"Sure of that?"

"Yes. I'm sure. He doesn't know Francine's dead."

"Did you call anybody besides me?"

"No."

Runyon glanced at his watch. Four forty. "What time does Darby usually get home?"

"I don't know. . . ."

"When you were married to him—what time then?"

"No set time. He usually called if he was going to be later than six. Oh, God, I don't want to be here when he comes." She gripped Runyon's arm. "Jake, do we have to call the police? Can't you just take Bobby and me away from here?"

He could, sure. Leave the door open, let Darby find Francine's body. Call the law from Bryn's house, or not call them at all, on the slim hope Darby and the police would assume an intruder had killed Francine. But running out, pretending, lying, were always bad ideas. Always ended up making a bad situation even worse.

"You know I can't do that," he said.

"Just Bobby, then. I don't care what happens to me. . . ."

"But I do. There's no place to take him and even if there was—"

"His doctor. His nose should be looked at, he could have other injuries."

"You said he was all right."

"Jake . . ."

"We stay right here, all three of us. I'll request an EMT unit for Bobby."

"I should've taken him to the doctor myself. But I was so upset, I wasn't thinking clearly. . . ."

"Bryn, listen to me." He waited until her eyes focused on him. "You're certain Francine was the one who picked up the knife?"

"Yes, I told you. She would've stabbed *me* if I hadn't grabbed her wrist."

"All right. Then you acted in self-defense. Bobby can verify that she hit him in the face—"

"No. I don't want him involved."

"He's already involved."

"He won't talk about the abuse, you know that." Bryn sucked in a breath, released it. "Will the police arrest me?"

Yeah, they would. This was Francine's home, there was no witness to corroborate what had happened in the kitchen, and the fact that Bryn had delayed reporting the crime by calling Runyon instead of 911 all mitigated against her; the cops wouldn't have any other choice. They'd book her on a 187 PC—the unlawful killing of a human being with malice aforethought. The initial charge in a case like this was almost always the most severe, justified or not.

Runyon said, "Don't worry about that now. When they get here, be polite but don't volunteer any information. Tell them you'll answer all their questions when you have your lawyer present. Understand?"

"Yes, but my lawyer only does family law—"

"I'll get you a criminal defense attorney. When you see him tell him everything you told me, exactly as it happened. Don't withhold anything."

"All right. Whatever you say."

"Sit down while I make the calls."

"I have to check on Bobby."

"Go ahead then."

Runyon watched her disappear through a doorway on the other side of the room. Then he flipped his cell phone open. He knew a couple of SFPD's homicide inspectors, and Bill's longtime poker buddy, Jack Logan, was an assistant chief whom he'd had some dealings with as well. But it wouldn't be a good idea to try personalizing this; that kind of approach could backfire. Better to just make a standard 911 call. He identified himself to the operator, briefly explained the situation, and requested an EMT unit for a child with minor injuries.

The best criminal attorney he knew from his short time in San Francisco was a tough old veteran named Thomas Dragovich. Runyon called Dragovich's law office, caught him in, and explained the situation in clipped sentences. Dragovich agreed to represent Bryn and reiterated what Runyon had told her, that she wasn't to answer any questions without him being present; said he'd be at the Hall of Justice to consult with her as soon as she was processed through the system. There wasn't much else Dragovich could do until she was arraigned, and that wasn't likely to happen for seventy-two hours. The police could hold her that long while they investigated and turned whatever evidence they'd gathered over to the DA's office.

After Runyon clicked off, he went quickly through the hallway door and down to where the bedrooms were. Bryn's low-pitched, crooning voice led him to the last of them: "It's going to be all right, baby. It's going to be all right. You didn't do anything wrong, it was all just a bad dream. Don't think about it, forget it ever happened. It's going to be all right."

The door was open; Runyon stepped through. Boy's bedroom overstuffed with the kind of material possessions a busy and overindulgent father lavishes on his son in place of quality time and genuine affection. Bryn was sitting beside Bobby on the double bed, the boy lying on his back with one hand limp on his middle, the other holding an ice pack to the center of his face. The T-shirt and Levi's he wore were clean, blood free. His eyes were open, starey, looking ceilingward while his mother talked to him.

She didn't hear Runyon come in, didn't know he was there until he made a small noise at the door. The noise startled her. She stopped crooning, bit her lip, glanced at him, then reached up to smooth a palm across Bobby's forehead. He took no notice of the gesture; the starey eyes were motionless, the lids unblinking.

Runyon said, "Your attorney's name is Thomas Dragovich. One of the best. You'll see him later at the Hall of Justice."

"Thank you." Solemn, formal.

Runyon moved over to the bed, leaned down for a closer look at the boy. Bobby's nose, visible under the ice pack, didn't look too bad—a little swollen, but not bleeding anymore. A Band-Aid covered the cut on his left cheek. The brown eyes flicked toward Runyon, but only for a moment; a single blink and they went starey again. Aware but nonresponsive. Reaction to the new abuse, Bryn's fight with Whalen—a retreat into himself, his own private hiding place.

Bryn said, "Don't try to talk to him, Jake. Please."

He nodded. "You want to wait in here?"

"Yes. Just the two of us."

"Okay."

Runyon left the room, went back down the hall. He was nearing the doorway to the living room when he heard the sounds—the front door opening, somebody coming in. He quickened his step, passed through into the living room. And pulled up short, because he wasn't looking at police officers or EMTs.

"You," Robert Darby said, staring back at him. "What the fuck are you doing in my home?"

14

JAKE RUNYON

Lousy timing, dammit. Another few minutes and the law would be here and they'd be the ones to break the news to Darby. Now Runyon would have to do it. And it was bound to make a bad situation even worse.

Runyon made a slow advance, his hands spread in front of him. "Take it easy, Mr. Darby. Bryn's here, too—she's in with Bobby."

"Bryn? She has no more right in my home than you do." Glowering, glancing around. "Where's Francine?"

"There's been some trouble."

". . . What do you mean, trouble?"

"An accident, pretty bad. The police are on the way."

Darby was a big man, jowly and going soft around the middle, but he had one of those faces that make some lawyers better than others in a courtroom: smooth, tight, unreadable, his feelings hidden behind a pair of piercing gray eyes. He stared at Runyon as if he were a hostile witness who had just made an outrageous statement on the stand.

"What kind of accident? What are you telling me?"

"Maybe you'd better sit down—"

"Answer my question. What's happened here?"

No way to soften it. "Your fiancée's dead, Mr. Darby."

"Dead." As if the word didn't compute. "Francine?"

"Yes. I'm sorry."

"How, for God's sake? What happened?"

"An accident. Stabbed."

"Stabbed." Another word that didn't seem to compute. Then, in a sudden angry flare, "*You*, you son of a bitch?"

"No."

"Who, then? Who stabbed her?"

"She's been abusing your son. Hit him in the face today, bloodied his nose, cut his cheek—"

"Who stabbed her!"

"She did it herself, accidentally. She—"

Dark blood suffused Darby's face. He came up on his toes in a forward lean, his lips peeled back from his teeth. Runyon set himself; no matter how upset the man was, he wasn't going to get anywhere near Bryn. But Darby didn't charge him. Stood breathing hard, struggling with his control.

Half a dozen beats. Then, "Where? When?"

"Here. Less than an hour ago."

"You see it?"

"No. I've only been here a few minutes."

"Then how do you know what happened?"

"Bryn told me. Francine attacked her—"

"I don't believe it. She's lying."

"No. I told you, Francine has been abusing your son. She fractured his arm, among other—"

"Where is she? Where's Francine?"

"Kitchen. But you don't want to go in there."

"The hell I don't."

Darby moved then, jerkily, heading for the swing door. Runyon called after him, "Don't touch anything," an automatic warning that he regretted as soon as the words were out. Insensitive. And Darby wasn't listening anyway. Runyon could have followed to make sure the warning was heeded, but he didn't; he was enough of an intruder already.

A sound behind him turned his head. Bryn was standing in the hall doorway. "I was listening," she said. "Why did he have to come home *now*?"

"Go back in with Bobby."

"Where are the police? Why don't they get here?"

"Any minute. Stay in the bedroom."

Too late. Darby reappeared, walking in a flat-footed, not quite steady way; his face was ashen, the only outward indication of what he was feeling. When he saw Bryn, he said in a thin, strained voice, "You crazy bitch, what've you done?" and this time he did come stalking forward.

Runyon got in Darby's way. Body block, legs spread, shoulder lifted and turned, keeping his arms down in front of him. Lay hands on a lawyer in a situation like this and it could be construed as assault. But it didn't come to anything physical. Darby pulled up just before there was contact, so close Runyon could smell the minty odor of his breath, and glared past him at Bryn in the hallway.

She said, "Robert, I'm sorry, I never meant for this to happen—"

"You'll pay for it, count on that."

Runyon said, low and even, "Back off, Mr. Darby."

Darby's gaze shifted back to him. He drew a heavy breath,

retreated a step to put a little distance between them—but only the one step. "I want to see my son."

Couldn't deny him that. "All right. Bryn, come out here."

"No. Robert, leave the boy alone, please. . . ."

"Shut up, damn you. Shut up!"

Bryn made a low, anguished sound.

And that was when the first blue wave rolled in.

The pair of uniformed officers, one male, one female, didn't have time to do much except add to the tension. It wasn't until the arrival of the team of homicide inspectors a short while later that things calmed down. Runyon didn't know either of them, quietly professional black men in their fifties, Farley and Crabtree. They'd been partners for a long time, visited crime scenes a lot bloodier and more chaotic than this one; you could tell that from the practiced way they took charge.

They had their look at the body, turned the kitchen over to the forensic team that had come in with them, then started their Q & A. Bryn first, after which her rights were read to her, then Runyon, then Darby, who settled down once he realized his accusations against her were having no effect. At first, foolishly, she disobeyed instructions by trying to explain what had happened and to justify her actions. Runyon warned her to wait until she'd consulted with her attorney, and after that she kept quiet. He answered the questions put to him truthfully but impersonally and with as little detail as possible. Otherwise he, too, kept his own counsel.

The EMTs showed up finally, late because it hadn't been an emergency call. The verdict on Bobby was slight cartilage damage to his nose, minor facial injury, and suffering from shock. Hospitalization not required, a visit to the family doctor recommended if the shock symptoms persisted. Darby vehemently denied that Francine had been abusing the boy; Bryn, with Runyon's backup, just as vehemently insisted she had. One of the inspectors, Crabtree, tried to talk to the boy; so did Darby. Neither of them got anywhere.

The whole thing took little more than an hour. End result: Bobby was allowed to remain in his father's charge and Bryn was handcuffed and turned over to the pair of uniforms for transport to the women's jail facility at the Hall of Justice. Runyon managed a few words with her before she was led away, to let her know what he was going to do. A short time afterward, the inspectors allowed him to leave on his promise to appear at the Hall of Justice the next day to sign a formal statement.

There was nothing more he could do now. Bail would probably be set high at her arraignment—it usually was in a homicide case, no matter what arguments the defense attorney put forth—but whatever the amount, Runyon wouldn't let it be a problem. Abe Melikian owed him a favor—he'd saved the bondsman a bundle on the Madison case a short while back—and he'd call it in when the time came.

Runyon was too jittery, too jammed up inside, to face his empty apartment. He fed his Ford a tankful of gas, took himself out of the city to the south and on up to Skyline. He drove all the way down the spine of the Coast Range to the intersection with Highway 84, took 84 over to the coast and its juncture with Highway 1 at San Gregorio. Dark, winding, forest-flanked roads, fog draped, neither of them with much traffic. The kind of long, semirelaxing night ride he'd been prone to before Bryn came into his life.

But the drive didn't ease him down any on this night. Didn't banish the doubts that kept crawling like bugs through his mind.

Had Bryn told the whole truth about Francine's death?

He was pretty sure she'd never lied to him before; he didn't want to believe she was lying now. Yet something didn't quite ring true about her story. It seemed plausible enough on the surface, but when he replayed it in his mind it struck a faintly rehearsed chord, like half a hundred similar tales he'd listened to that had been proven partly or completely false during his years on the Seattle force.

What she'd said about Francine on Saturday echoed darkly in his memory.

I don't blame Bobby for wishing her dead. I'd like to kill her myself. . . .

Damn her! She'll keep right on hurting him, and the next time . . . the next time . . . I won't let it happen. I won't.

Accident as she claimed, end result of a struggle after Francine picked up the knife? Or had Bryn been the one to pick it up, use it deliberately—maybe even gone to the flat with that idea in mind?

Self-defense—or murder?

15

Friday was what the media refers to as an eventful news day. And like much of what the media reports, the news that came my way was neither pleasant nor particularly enlightening.

The first piece came from Jake Runyon. He and Tamara were having a stand-up conference in her office when I walked into the agency. The grim set of their faces foretold the fact that I was not going to like the subject of their discussion. Right. I didn't like it one damn bit.

"Police are holding Bryn on a homicide charge," Runyon told me.

"Jesus. What happened?"

"Party to the death of the woman who's been abusing her son."

"Woman? You said the boy's father was the abuser."

"Turned out I was wrong. His fiancée, Francine Whalen."

Runyon couldn't seem to keep still; he took a restless turn to the door and back, stood then with his feet moving in place like a man on one of those treadmill machines as he explained the situation.

I said when he was done, "Mother reacting to an assault on her son by a woman with a documentable history of violent abuse. Justifiable. Dragovich is a good man—he'll get her off."

"That's what I keep telling myself. But there's only her word Whalen was the one who picked up the knife. And Whalen's history is only documentable if one of her other victims steps forward. Darby's still in denial—he keeps insisting Whalen never laid a hand on Bobby."

"So it all hinges on the boy."

"And getting him to talk won't be easy. His father's liable to do or say something to drive him deeper into his shell."

Bleak, all right. But still a long way from hopeless. "You need some time off to deal with this, Jake?"

"I don't know yet. I might."

"Take as much as you need. And if there's anything else we can do . . ."

Runyon nodded, his feet still moving, and scraped a hand over his slablike face. He'd shaved this morning, but it had been a hasty and probably distracted job; there were little patches of stubble on his chin and one cheek. His eyes were blood flecked, the bags under them as gray as duffles. He hadn't slept much last night, if he'd slept at all.

"I'll let you know how it goes," he said, and he was gone.

Tamara said, "That man's had a miserable damn life. Everybody he cares about . . . bam, something bad happens."

"Yeah."

"You think he's in love with Bryn?"

"Hard to tell what Jake's feelings are. But I wouldn't be surprised."

"Then Dragovich better get her off."

"He will if anybody can."

"Life's a bitch sometimes," Tamara said. She let out a breathy sigh, then sat down at her desk and punched up a file on her Mac. "Might as well get back to work."

"Might as well."

"Rose O'Day," she said.

"Pardon?"

"The old woman who rented a room from McManus, the one the neighbor told you about."

"Oh, right. What about her?"

What about her was the second bit of the day's news.

"I did some checking last night," Tamara said. "Lots of history until three years ago, but nothing since. No current residence in the Bay Area or Michigan or anywhere else. No death record. No brother in Saginaw, or other living family members."

"So it seems McManus lied to Mrs. Hightower."

"Seems?"

"If the neighbor's memory is accurate after three years. It's hearsay in any case."

"Well, that's not all I came up with. When the woman's husband died five years ago, his insurance policy paid her a death benefit of fifty thousand. She also inherited some rural property his brother willed to him in West Marin worth twice that much."

"So?"

"There's no record of her investing the fifty K, so chances are she stuck it in her bank account. And that account's still active."

"You sure about that?"

"Yep. I couldn't find out how much is in the account without some serious security breaching."

"Always a don't-cross line. Local bank?"

"B of A branch at Embarcadero Center."

"Does the Marin property still belong to her?"

"No record of it being sold."

"Taxes current or delinquent?"

"Paid up to date."

"So we've got two possibilites," I said. "One is that she still resides somewhere in or near the city. It's not inconceivable that an elderly woman living alone in a rented room could fall under the radar."

"You believe that? I don't."

"I didn't say I believed it. I said it was one possibility. The other—"

"—is that McManus killed Rose O'Day to get control of her assets. That's the one I believe."

"You don't necessarily have to commit murder to get your hands on a person's assets."

"No? Why else would she lie about what happened to O'Day?"

"If anything happened to her."

"Well, something happened to Virden. One disappearance, one probable disappearance—"

"Make that possible."

"Okay, possible. But I don't buy the coincidence. We're pretty sure McManus is an ID thief, right? Steal one woman's ID, and that woman disappears. Stands to reason she'd steal another woman's money and make *her* disappear if she had the chance."

"Granted," I said. "But it's still only conjecture. I hate to keep harping on this, but we need clear-cut evidence of wrong-doing before we can act and we don't have any. Not where

McManus is concerned, not where Virden is concerned, not where Rose O'Day is concerned."

Tamara had that stubborn bulldog look, the kind I'd seen before and not just on her; it had stared back at me from a mirror more than a few times. "I've got an idea how we might get some," she said.

"Okay, let's hear it."

"Get inside the McManus house and check it out, check out the property. Got to be something incriminating there."

"Don't tell me you're advocating B and E?"

"Uh-uh. McManus rents rooms, doesn't she?"

"To elderly people. She's no dummy and she's already suspicious. Probably wouldn't even let you in the house."

"Wasn't thinking of me. Alex. He's forty-six, but he can pass for a few years older. Old enough."

"Same objection applies."

"Worth a try, isn't it?"

I thought about it. There were other arguments against the idea, but none strong enough to shoot it down. Pretty soon I said, "Might work. If the room's still for rent—the sign was down when I was there yesterday. And if McManus has no prejudice against Latinos. He'll have to be damn careful if he does get in."

"You know Alex—he's always careful."

"Okay, then. Give him a call."

"Already did. He's on his way."

One jump ahead of me, as usual. "There's another tack we can take," I said. "Find out the names of some of McManus's other roomers, track down their present whereabouts. Maybe one of them has some information we can use. What's the real estate outfit that handles her lease?"

"Barber and Associates. Offices on Sansome downtown."

"You have the agent's name?"

"No, but I can get it."

"Do that. I'll make a second canvass of McManus's neighbors, too—have another talk with Selma Hightower."

Tamara favored me with a satisfied grin. "Now that's what I'm talkin' about," she said.

Alex Chavez had come and gone, fully briefed, and I was on my way out when the third piece of news arrived. This one came in a text message from Felice Johnson, Tamara's friend and contact at SFPD. Tamara had asked her for a personal BOLO for David Virden's Porsche Cayman, and the car had just turned up—or what was left of it had—in an alley out near the Cow Palace. A couple of message exchanges later, we had the details.

Found abandoned, stripped down to the frame. The officers who'd spotted it were regulars on that beat; their report said it hadn't been there when they made their first pass through the area shortly past midnight. Driver's window smashed, the ignition hot-wired. No signs of blood, interior or exterior. Nothing to indicate what might have happened to Virden.

I said, "The ignition hot-wire pretty much rules out a carjacking."

"Tells me it was abandoned twice," Tamara said. "First time on some dark street near the projects. Wouldn't've lasted more than an hour after midnight. Sweet set of wheels like that's a prime target for car boosters. Then hot-wired and driven over to that alley and stripped."

"McManus and Carson again."

"Who else? One of 'em drove it out of Dogpatch sometime Tuesday; the other one followed in the SUV to bring her back."

"That's one explanation," I said. "Another is that the first boost was by somebody in Dogpatch or elsewhere."

"Car thieves don't hang on to a ride three days before they strip it."

"Nonprofessionals might. Joyriders, gangbangers."

"Then what happened to Virden?"

"Hit over the head, robbed, the body dumped where it hasn't been found yet."

"By joyriders or gangbangers? I don't buy it. McManus and Carson whacked him, all right."

"How do you suppose they managed it? Big healthy guy, mad as hell, and two smallish women."

"And one killer dog. Sicced that Rottweiler, what's his name, Thor, on him, ripped his throat out."

"Uh-huh. Which would mean blood all over the place. One hell of a job cleaning it up."

"Not if it happened outside."

"Where his screams could be heard a block away."

Tamara made a face at me.

I said, "This isn't getting us anywhere. Time to call Judith LoPresti, let her know about the Porsche being found. Police probably wouldn't have notified her yet and it's better if she hears it from us."

"You going to say anything about McManus and Carson?"

"That we might be dealing with a couple of identity thieves who also happen to be Madam Bluebeards? Not hardly. She'll be upset enough as it is."

16

JAKE RUNYON

When he left the agency he drove down to the Hall of Justice to have a talk with Bryn. Only he didn't get to do that because they wouldn't let him see her. She'd been put into Administrative Segregation for her own protection the night before, which meant no visitors except for her attorney. Why the hell would they AdSeg her? Nobody would tell Runyon the reason.

Maybe Dragovich could. Runyon wanted to talk to him anyway, in person, to get his take on her legal situation. He called Dragovich's law office to make sure he was in before driving downtown.

The doubts about Bryn's story still plagued him. He'd been over it and over it and still he couldn't quite put his finger on what rang false. Part of it had to do with the sudden shift in her emotional makeup: frantic, nearly hysterical, when she'd called him, calm when he'd arrived at Darby's flat. The twenty-five minutes it'd taken him to get to the Marina was time enough for her to regain control, yet her calm hadn't had the residue of shock and terror in it. What he'd seen, sensed, was a mixture of resignation and determination, as if in the interim she'd made some sort of accommodation or decision. Possible he'd read her reactions wrong, but his cop's instincts said he hadn't.

There were other things, too. Her account of what'd happened seemed a little too pat, as if some or all of it had been quickly made up and then gone over and refined several times before his arrival. And why had she volunteered information to the homicide inspectors when she'd been warned not to? There was something else, too, something off-key she'd said or done before Darby and the police showed up that kept eluding him.

It all came down to a measure of premeditation: Bryn had gone to the flat to confront Francine, lost it when she saw Bobby hurt again, and in the heat of the fight that followed picked up the kitchen knife and stabbed the woman. That would explain Bryn's near hysteria when she called; the aftermath of violence, even anticipated violence, throws most people into a panicked state. It would also explain the calm: resignation once she gathered herself, then the decision, the determination, to alter her account to protect herself.

But the problem with that was, Bryn was neither a liar nor a violent person. He couldn't see her willfully taking anyone's life, even a woman she hated as much as Francine Whalen. Or fashioning a net of lies to cover up a homicide. Totally out of character.

Or was it? How well did he really know her? Only a short time since they'd met; only a few weeks since they'd become intimate both physically and emotionally. She was complicated, high-strung, damaged by the stroke, her husband's betrayal, the custody loss of her son. He wasn't a shrink, couldn't probe down into the psyche of a woman like Bryn. Just wasn't equipped. The trouble he'd had dealing with his own demons was proof of that.

He *could* be wrong about her. Didn't want to believe he was, but the possibility was still there. Wouldn't go away until he knew exactly what had happened in Robert Darby's flat yesterday afternoon.

Dragovich's law office was on Grove Street close to City Hall. As successful as his criminal law practice was, he didn't believe in spending money on jazzing up his workplace. His private office had the usual shelves of law books and an over-sized desk, but there were none of the expensive trappings— leather furniture, polished wood paneling, mirrors, paintings, wet bar—that some high-powered attorneys went in for. Strictly functional. Runyon didn't much like lawyers as a general rule—too many of them were self-promoting, profiteering sharks—but Dragovich was an exception. A man as straightforward and businesslike as his surroundings.

In his late forties and small in stature, not much more than five eight and a hundred and forty pounds; even with his chair jacked up high, the desk dwarfed him. Thinning sandy hair, a beak of a nose, a pointy chin. Habitually he wore a gray suit, a pale blue shirt, and a striped red tie, a kind of signatory outfit like the TV lawyer Matlock. Except that no matter what time of day you saw Dragovich, his shirt collar was unbuttoned, the knot in his tie was loosened, and his suit had a rumpled look. The compensation for all of that was his voice—deep, booming, commanding. He used it to maximum effect in a courtroom.

Runyon was admitted promptly to the attorney's private office. Dragovich shook his hand, waved him to a client's chair. As soon as they were both seated, Runyon said, "I just came from the Hall. Do you know why they AdSeg'd Bryn?"

"Yes. It happened after I consulted with her last night—I saw her again early this morning. I wish you'd told me about her stroke."

"What does that have to do with it?"

"Badly agitated after she was booked because she wasn't allowed to cover the damaged side of her face."

"Why wasn't she?"

"Jail rules. No scarves—the standard suicide concern. She begged for a towel, but the matrons wouldn't give her one for the same reason. While she and I talked she tried to cover her face with toilet paper."

Toilet paper. Jesus Christ.

"After I left her," Dragovich said, "apparently some of the other prisoners made fun of her condition and she had what the matrons called a temporary breakdown. They were afraid she might harm herself—that's why she was AdSeg'd."

Runyon's hands bunched into fists. As sensitive as Bryn was about her face, the humiliation she'd felt must've been acute. The thought of her being harassed by women without conscience or compassion was galling.

"Is she all right now?"

"Better, yes. Resigned. And very concerned about her son."

"But still segregated. How long before I can see her?"

"I wasn't given a time line."

"Not until her arraignment?"

"It's possible."

"Is there anything you can do to get me in to see her?"

"You mean in my presence?"

"Alone, preferably."

Dragovich gave him a long, shrewd look. "Is there a specific reason you want to see her alone? If there is, you'd be well advised to tell me what it is."

What could he say? That he was afraid she was either lying or telling half-truths? That he was afraid she might actually be guilty of the unlawful killing of a human being with malice aforethought?

"Personal reasons," he said. "You already know everything I know about Francine Whalen's death."

"I hope so."

"Will you do what you can to get me permission?"

"Of course. But I'm not in a position of strength on this issue."

Runyon changed the subject. "Concerned about her son, you said. Bobby's welfare, what his father might say or do to him?"

"Yes."

"She has good reason."

"I don't know Robert Darby, except by reputation." The attorney's mouth quirked wryly. "There seems to be some question as to whether he upholds the highest standards of our profession."

"Have you talked to him yet?"

"I have a call in to him. Of course he's under no obligation to speak to me at this time. He may decide to wait until Mrs. Darby is arraigned."

"If he doesn't return your call, can you find out how the boy's doing some other way?"

"The inspectors in charge should know. I'll check with them when they come on duty this afternoon."

Runyon asked Dragovich what he thought Bryn's chances were. Unlike some criminal defense attorneys, he was never overconfident; cautious optimism was the limit of his pretrial position on any case. It was likely that the judge at Bryn's arraignment would uphold the homicide charge and the DA's office would prosecute, in which case Dragovich would advise her to plead not guilty. The DA might or might not opt to proceed on the first-degree charge, depending on how convinced he was that willful premeditation could be proven. Dragovich's best guess was that it would be knocked down to either second degree or manslaughter, both of which offered the DA a better chance of conviction.

In any event, and as Runyon had surmised, self-defense would be difficult to prove without a witness to Whalen's death. But still it seemed the best option under the circumstances. Juries were notoriously unpredictable, but they tended to side with a defendant mother in a homicide case involving child abuse—if the abuse was proven to their satisfaction. Testimony by the victim was the best way to accomplish jury sympathy, but when Dragovich had broached the subject to Bryn this morning she'd been adamant against it. Didn't want Bobby put through any more pain and suffering, she'd said. Even if she changed her mind, they'd have her ex-husband to contend with.

If Bobby didn't take the stand, then it was up to Bryn and Runyon to do what they could to verify the scope and nature of the boy's injuries. Whalen's history of violent behavior would have to be established as well. Runyon named Gwen Whalen, Kevin Dinowski, and Charlene Kepler as witnesses who could be subpoenaed to testify. Tricky business, Dragovich said, if that was the way they had to proceed. How much those individuals would be willing to admit to under oath and how much of their testimony would be ruled admissible was problematic.

"Odds for acquittal at fifty-fifty, then," Runyon said.

"Slightly better than that, I'd say. Based on the facts we have now and contingent on witness cooperation."

Based on the facts they had now. All the facts? One way or another, he had to find out.

17

ALEX CHAVEZ

He liked dogs. Elena liked dogs. His kids and his in-laws liked dogs. Even Elmo, the wirehaired terrier, liked other dogs.

But Chavez didn't like Thor, not one little bit.

Neither did Elmo.

As soon as the terrier spotted the big Rottweiler, the wiry hair on Elmo's back rippled up and he whined and scooted around behind Chavez, wrapping the leash around his legs, and stood there quivering. Thor didn't move, didn't make a sound. But those yellow eyes of his . . . *Dios,* it was like looking into the eyes of a demon.

The woman—Jane Carson, from the boss's description—didn't seem any happier to see him and Elmo than the Rotweiller did. He was already halfway up the driveway when she came out of the house carrying a cardboard box; the gate stood open, an invitation to walk right in. The hatch on the Ford Explorer parked there was raised and she quickly slid the box inside as he approached. No welcoming smile, no expression at all in her bright blue eyes. She was wearing dark-colored sweats, a headband around her short blond hair.

He said through a wary smile, "You ought to put that pooch of yours on a chain. He looks pretty mean."

"He's not. He's friendly and well trained."

"Elmo doesn't think so."

"Elmo?"

"My terrier here. See the way he's shaking? Scared to death."

"If you want to board him—"

"That's one reason I'm here," Chavez said. "The other is, I'm looking for a place to live and the bartender down at The Dog Hole says you have a room to rent."

"Well, he's wrong; we don't."

"Already rented?"

"Yes, already rented."

"You wouldn't have another available, would you? I mean, I'm kind of desperate for a place and this neighborhood is real convenient to my job—"

"One is all we have." She flicked a glance at Elmo. "And we're not taking any new dogs right now."

"No? How come?"

She was making an effort to hang on to her cool. Irritation leaked through anyway. She said as she wiped a thin beading of sweat off her forehead, "We're full up."

Chavez moved a little forward and to one side, dragging Elmo with him and keeping a watchful eye on the Rottweiler, so he could get a better look at the Explorer's interior through the open hatch. Full of boxes, piles of clothing on hangers, odds and ends.

"Looks like you're moving," he said.

"What?" Sharp look. "No. Donations for Goodwill."

He showed her the smile Elena had labeled Butter Wouldn't Melt in Your Mouth. His wife had a name for all his smiles and grins; the one he liked best and used on her three or four times a week was his Watch Out Tonight, *Querida* leer. "Spring housecleaning, huh?" he said.

"Yes, that's right. Now if you'll excuse me—"

"When do you think you'll be ready again?"

". . . Ready for what?"

"To take in more dogs."

"Come back the first of next month."

"Be okay if I have a look around now?"

Bought him a narrow-eyed stare. "What?"

"At the kennels. Make sure it's the right place for Elmo."

"No, it wouldn't be okay. Can't you see I'm busy?" She turned abruptly, started back toward the house.

Chavez took the opportunity for a squint down the driveway. Couldn't see much except part of a wire-fenced dog run and an outbuilding behind it that had to be the kennels. He said quickly, "How about I leave my name and phone number? In case the room opens up."

She stopped and turned, no longer even trying to hide her annoyance. "There's no point in that. The tenant we have now plans on an indefinite stay. Now will you please go away?" That last was neither a request nor a dismissal—she said it like a threat.

He'd pushed it as far as he could. Anything further and she'd make a real issue of it. Might even be suspicious as it was. He put on his Piqued and Pouty smile and said, with just the right amount of edge, "Sure, lady, whatever you say. I don't think I'd have liked living here anyway."

Nothing from her.

Chavez took the terrier back down the drive. Elmo was relieved; by the time they reached the street, he'd quit shivering and his stubby tail was wagging again. The woman, Carson, had disappeared back into the house.

His dependable old Dodge was parked on 20th Street, one house down. He ran Elmo into the backseat, slid himself into the front. Drove off, circled half a dozen blocks, and then rolled back along Minnesota to where he had a pretty clear view of the McManus house and the SUV from that direction. Carson was still inside, the driveway empty—but she'd been back out at least once, because now the front gate was closed against further visitors. Chavez eased over to the curb, shut off the engine. Then he slouched down low on the seat, shifted his behind until he was comfortable, and reported in to Tamara.

She wasn't disappointed that he hadn't been able to get into the house. Matter of fact, there was an undertone of excitement in her voice when she said, "So they're moving out?"

"Sure looks that way. They're still loading up the SUV, both of them now—the other one just showed."

"Leaving as soon as they're done, you think?"

"Could be. Carson seemed pretty anxious to get rid of me. Want me to run a tail?"

"Oh yeah. Even if only one of them leaves. Did Carson get a good look at your car?"

"Doubt it. She didn't see me coming and she was already in the house when I drove away."

"Good. Keep me posted."

Chavez said he would and clicked off.

"Elmo," he said then, "I shouldn't have dragged you into this. Seemed like a good idea when I left the agency, but now you're stuck with me. Might be a while before either of us gets home again."

Elmo didn't seem to mind. He stretched up and licked the back of Chavez's neck.

Most investigators hated stakeouts, the waiting, the downtime, but Alex Chavez wasn't one of them. Elena claimed it was because he was basically lazy and would rather sit on his fat *culo* than do anything else. But she was only teasing him. She knew he had more energy than most men his age, knew it better than anybody because of how often he demonstrated it to her in bed. Besides, his *culo* wasn't fat.

The reason stakeouts didn't bother him was because he liked to listen to the radio. The Dodge had a brand-new battery, so he didn't have to worry about running down the juice by playing the radio with the engine off. It wasn't music he listened to, not that he didn't like music. Elena was a big fan of traditional Latin ballads, the kids were into salsa and hip-hop and Hannah Montana; his preference was Garth Brooks. A shame to his heritage, Elena said—more of her teasing. But even a steady diet of Brooks made Chavez yawn and put him to sleep.

No, what he listened to was right-wing hate radio.

That was the correct term. Limbaugh, Beck, the rest of them—a pack of greed-driven racist hatemongers hiding behind the cloak of patriotism. He'd been assaulted by that kind of crap all his life, on and off the radio and television. Down in El Centro when he was growing up and before and after he joined the county sheriff's department, even up here in liberal

San Francisco. Wetback, spic, greaser—he'd heard all the epi-
thets dozens of times and been called worse to his face. Heard
"close the borders," "go back to Mexico where you belong,"
"keep America safe for Americans." Well, the Chavezes were
as American as Limbaugh and Beck, every one of them born
and raised in this country.

Elena, the rest of his family, didn't understand why he listened to the trash that came spewing over the airwaves. Wal-
lowed in it, they said. But he didn't look at it as wallowing.
Know your enemy, that was one reason he did it—what
they're saying, doing, thinking. Made it easier to deal with
the results of their rhetoric when he was confronted with it,
easier to keep his anger in check, easier to do his job.

The other reason was because it gave him a benign feeling
of superiority. Alex Chavez and the Chavez family were good,
God-fearing people who worked hard for what they had,
whose hearts were full of love, not hate. They were better
Christians, better role models, more honest believers in family values. Better Americans because they didn't try to tell
anybody else what to think and how to live their lives. Better
human beings. Knowing that, having it verified every time
he tuned in to one of the wing nut broadcasts, helped him
maintain his equilibrium and his essentially cheerful out-
look. Ironic, when you looked at it that way. A kind of justice
in it, too. The more the haters ranted and raved and spewed
their venom against minorities, the happier and prouder he
was that he'd been born one himself.

Limbaugh's diatribe today had to do with President Obama's
foreign-policy decisions and how the health-care reform law
was destroying the country. The usual garbage, regurgitated.
After a while Chavez only half-listened, because he'd heard it

so many times before he could have recited most of it himself, word for word.

Across the street Carson appeared one last time, carrying a couple of what looked to be Tiffany table lamps, found space for them inside, then closed the Explorer's hatch and disappeared into the house again. Otherwise nothing much happened for close to an hour. At the forty-minute mark Elmo gave out with his I Have to Go whine. Well, that figured. World's smallest dog bladder. Chavez slid out on the passenger side, let the terrier out, kept one eye on him while he sprayed the trunk of a sidewalk tree and the other on the house. One thing you could say for Elmo: he never dallied when he was doing his business, like some dogs did. Do it and get on with the important things, like munching a Milk-Bone and then curling up and going to sleep on the backseat.

Chavez was scanning through the radio dial, looking for one or another of Limbaugh's fellow garbagemen, when the wait came to a worthwhile end. The two women walked out of the house together, the Rottweiler with them on a leash. Not hurrying but not taking their time, either. Carson went down to open the gate while McManus prodded Thor in on the driver's side of the SUV. While she drove out to the street, Chavez fired up the Dodge. Carson closed the gate and hopped in on the passenger side; then the Explorer rolled out of the driveway.

And the chase was on.

Not that it was much of a chase at first. McManus was a cautious driver and there wasn't much traffic, so he hung back at a safe distance as she headed south on Third. She turned west on Cesar Chavez Street (named after a great man whose surname he was proud to share), bypassed the edge of the San

Jose Guerrero neighborhood where he lived, and went on up to Church Street. Right on Church, left on Clipper, up the hill to the intersection with Market, then left across Twin Peaks and down the west side on Portola Drive. He had a pretty good idea by then where they were going, and it wasn't to any Goodwill store.

He knew for sure he was right when the SUV turned down Sloat, then north on Nineteenth Avenue. While he waited two cars behind at a stoplight just beyond Stern Grove, he slid his cell phone into the hands-free device mounted on the dash and called Tamara to tell her McManus and Carson were on the move and likely heading for the Golden Gate Bridge.

18

My visit to Barber and Associates was unproductive. The agent in charge of the Dogpatch property lease was a middle-aged black woman named Royster; I got her to talk to me on the grounds that I was conducting a routine insurance investigation that peripherally involved R. L. McManus. Ms. Royster was unaware McManus was in the habit of subletting a room, but she didn't seem to be particularly concerned about it. She checked the lease agreement to determine if there was a clause forbidding sublets; there wasn't. Ms. McManus had been a model tenant, she said, always paying her rent on time, not once requesting repairs or improvements to the property, and making no complaint when the monthly nut was increased, as it had been twice in the seven years she'd lived there.

Ms. Royster knew nothing about McManus's background or personal life, other than the fact that her references had been impeccable. Knew nothing about Jane Carson, either. Even if there had been something in the file that might have been pertinent, she probably wouldn't have confided to me what it was. Privileged information.

The only new thing I learned from her—and it wasn't much—was that the owners of the house, an elderly couple now residing in Burlingame, had also operated a dog-boarding service on the property. The established existence of kennels and dog run was probably what had attracted McManus to it seven years ago.

The visit to Barber and Associates may have been wasted, but a second trip to Dogpatch wasn't. My first stop there, The Dog Hole, yielded a little info of the sort I was looking for—enough to put Tamara on the scent again.

The rail-thin elderly guy I'd spoken to the first time around occupied the same bar stool, sipping port and playing a quiet game of solitaire. Cheating at it, too: he switched a king and queen in a row of hearts as I sat down next to him. Lonely, bored, drinking just enough to maintain a mild sedative buzz—a man with nowhere else to go and nothing else to do, marking time.

He remembered me, he was grateful for the company, and my offer to stand him to another drink made him friendly and gregarious. His name was Frank Quarles, he said, and chuckled and tacked on a mild joke he'd probably told a few hundred times before: "My late wife used to say we was well named because we sure did have a lot of 'em. Quarrels, get it?"

I chuckled to let him know I'd gotten it, then told him I was still looking for the man in the photograph. He hadn't seen Virden since last Tuesday, he said. I eased the conversation around to McManus's roomers. Quarles couldn't recall any of the women, but when I brought up the old man Selma Hightower had mentioned, it struck a chord in his memory.

"Oh, sure, him," he said. "I'm seventy, but he was a real geezer. One foot in the grave and the other on a bar stool."

"He came here regularly, did he?"

"Pretty regular for a while. Two, three months."

"Then what happened?"

"Just stopped showing up. Figured he must've passed over."

"You spend much time with him?"

"Not much, no sir. Damn near deaf, so he kept pretty much to himself. Nice old bird, though. Wasn't above buying a round for the house now and then."

"Sounds like he had money."

"Must've. Wore this old black overcoat with a velvet collar. Made out of lamb's wool, he said." Quarles aimed a glance at the muscle-bound bartender, lowered his voice. "Drank good Scotch, too. Not the blended bar crap they serve here. Twelve-year-old single malt."

"Do you remember his name?"

"Well . . . it's been a while and my memory's not what it used to be." Up went the voice again. "Hey, Stan. You remember that old guy came in regular for a while last year? Drank single malt Scotch?"

"Glenlivet. What about him?"

"Remember his name?"

"Nope. My business is drinks, not names."

I said to Quarles, "Maybe another glass of port will help you dredge it up," and signaled to the bartender.

"Thank you, sir." Quarles closed his eyes, his face screwed up with effort. Pretty soon he opened them again and sighed and shook his head. "Just can't quite get it. Foreign name, that's all I can remember."

"He was a foreigner?"

"Not anymore. American citizen."

"What nationality?"

"Greek. Sure, I remember that now." Quarles took a sip of his port. "Came over here when he was a kid, made his money in the restaurant business. What the devil was his name? Papa something. No, it sounded like 'papa.'" Another sip, another frown that suddenly morphed into a smile. "Pappas. That's it, Pappas."

"First name?"

"Wasn't Greek. American. Wait, now . . . same as that actor, tall fella, played in a bunch of Westerns."

"John Wayne?"

"No sir, no, not the Duke. Famous, though, won an Oscar for that film about the lawyer and his family down south. Had 'bird' in the title . . ."

"*To Kill a Mockingbird.* Gregory Peck."

"That's it. Real fine actor. How could I forget *his* name?"

"Gregory, then—Gregory Pappas. You're sure?"

"Pretty sure. Yep, pretty sure."

I left Quarles smiling wistfully over what remained of his port and drove up 20th Street past the McManus house. Nobody around, the driveway empty, the *Room for Rent* sign still absent from the front fence. No sign of Alex Chavez's Dodge, either. Been here and gone—I wondered how he'd made out.

Selma Hightower wasn't home. At least, nobody answered the bell. I tried to recall which of the other neighbors had been cooperative on my first canvass, picked the likeliest of them, and was hoofing it around the corner on Minnesota Street when my cell phone went off.

Tamara. With news from Alex Chavez about McManus and Carson.

"If Alex can stay with them long enough, we'll have some idea of where they're going," she said when she'd relayed the gist of it. "Wherever it is, it's north out of the city."

"If he's right, they're heading for the bridge."

"Must be on it by now. He'd've called back if they'd turned off. Bet you they're running."

"Maybe. What do you think spooked them into it?"

"Us, our investigation."

"Virden's disappearance? If they're responsible, they went through a lot of trouble to cover it up and as far as they know they got away with it. Why cut and and run now?"

"They can't be sure we're not close to nailing their asses."

"Would that be enough reason for you to suddenly throw up everything and take off? Because somebody *might* be getting close? Running is an admission of guilt, you know that."

"What about the ID theft?"

"Minor crime compared to homicide or manslaughter. And hard to prove without a complaint being filed. Virden didn't call the law on them and neither did we. No, that's not it."

"Something to do with the property or the house? Like maybe a dead body that's starting to stink and they don't know what to do with it?"

"Jesus. You have a gruesome turn of mind sometimes."

"Well, that couldn't be what happened to Rose O'Day," Tamara said. "Over three years ago that she went missing. I wish we had the names of the more recent roomers."

"I've got one name," I said, and relayed what I'd been told about Gregory Pappas. "It may or may not be the man's right name. Quarles's memory is pretty shaky."

"I'm on it soon as we hang up. You still in Dogpatch?"

"Yes."

"Then how about you take a look around the McManus property? Perfect time for it, nobody there."

"I was thinking the same thing," I said. "But don't get too excited—I'm not about to break any laws."

"Just bend them a little, huh?"

I let that pass. "Get back to me right away if Alex has anything to report."

"Will do."

I left the car where it was, walked down to the McManus place. Trespassing on private property is a tricky business, but if the house was deserted I ought to be able to get away with a look around the exterior areas without making inquisitive neighbors or passersby suspicious. First rule: always act as if you belong. I opened the front gate and marched up onto the porch, not hurrying and not looking anywhere except straight ahead.

I leaned on the bell for half a minute. Empty echoes, as expected.

There was a path that angled over to the driveway. I followed that, again taking my time and trying to look purposeful, and turned down the driveway past a narrow side porch to the backyard. Beyond the house was a low building that ran most of the property's width, fronted by an empty wire-enclosed area—kennels and dog run. The rest of the yard was flower-bordered lawn crisscrossed by flagstone paths. The near end of the kennel building ended close to a tall neighboring fence; the entrance would be around on the far side. I headed in that direction. And that was when the frantic barking and whimpering started up inside.

At least two dogs, judging from the different cadences. Which meant what, if anything? Worth taking a look.

I opened the door, stuck my head inside. Canine odors mingled strongly with those of excrement—the kind of smells you get when a place hasn't been cleaned in a while. No lights on, the interior shrouded in gloom. I fumbled around on the walls, found a switch, and flipped it. A couple of low-wattage ceiling bulbs chased away the shadows, let me see two facing rows of wire-gated cages.

The barking and whimpering picked up as I moved along the cement floor between the cages. Two occupied, the rest empty. The bigger and louder of the dogs, the one doing the frantic barking, was a shelty that hurled himself against the gate as I passed. The other animal, smaller, short-haired, a breed I didn't recognize, lay on her belly with her front paws scrabbling at the cement floor; the whines and whimpers she was making had a frightened, mournful edge. It wasn't me that had them so frantic; it was hunger, thirst. The food and water dishes in both cages were empty, apparently long empty. And the cement floor in both was stained with urine, spotted with piles of feces.

Abandoned. Coldly, cruelly left here to starve.

Anger welled up in me, cold and hot at the same time. One thing I can't abide is the mistreatment of any living being, human or animal.

There was a utility table built against the wall farther along; a couple of twenty-pound bags of kibble sat on it, one half-empty and the other unopened. The empty cages were clean and contained water and food dishes. All of their doors, like the ones housing the shelty and the smaller dog, had thick wooden pegs for fasteners. I got clean dishes out of two of them, filled two with kibble, the others with water from a spigot alongside the table, and replaced them in the empty cages.

The shelty was still barking and frantically throwing himself against the mesh, but he didn't look mean. And wasn't. He bounced up against me when I opened his cage, let me take hold of his collar. He'd seen where I put the food and water, all but dragged me into the first of those cages, and immediately began wolfing the kibble. The smaller dog, a female, was harder to transfer. She cringed away from me, cowered shaking against the outer wall. I had to drag her out of there, into the other clean cage and up to the two bowls. She went for the water first, with wary eye shifts in my direction as I backed out and repegged the door.

There wasn't anything else I could do for the dogs now. They'd be all right until I could get the SPCA out after I was through here.

Outside, I sucked cold air for several seconds to clear my sinuses of the kennel stench. The windows in the bordering houses all looked empty—no nosy neighbors to wonder what I was doing on the property. I went first to the rear entrance, still trying to look as if I belonged here. A screen door was unlocked, but the hardwood door inside it was secure.

Up the driveway, then to the side porch, up the stairs to the door. I expected this one to be locked, too, but it wasn't. The knob turned under my hand and the door eased inward a couple of inches. According to Chavez's report to Tamara, this was the door McManus and Carson had used to haul their belongings out to the SUV; they'd been in such a hurry they'd neglected to lock it before leaving. Or hadn't cared enough to bother.

If I went inside I'd no longer be bending the law; I'd be breaking it. From illegal trespass to unlawful entry. Chances were I wouldn't find anything anyway. On the other hand, there was always the possibility they'd forgotten or overlooked something incriminating. I'd never know for sure unless I looked.

Well?

The hell with propriety, I thought. McManus and Carson were guilty of Christ knew how many crimes, and the only one we had any real evidence of was negligent cruelty to a couple of boarded dogs. All I was doing standing out here was wasting time and running the risk of calling attention to myself.

I shoved the door open and walked in.

This was the part of the house they'd used for Canine Customers. Combination storage and supply room: more bags of dog food, extra dishes, a couple of carrying cages, leashes hanging from wall pegs. And a stack of moving cartons near the door. I opened one of them. Clothing, odds and ends. Left here because there was no more room in the SUV? Or did McManus and Carson intend to come back from wherever they were heading for another load?

I went through an open doorway at the far end. Office. Desk, a couple of cabinets, cords and wires where a computer and printer, both now missing, had been hooked up. The cabinet and desk drawers were open and there was a scatter of papers over the desk and floor: they'd done their packing in a hurry. I picked up several papers at random for a quick look.

Paid customer invoices, paid utility bills, and the like. What was left in the drawers was more of the same. No income records, no bank statements, nothing pertaining to individual or professional finances. No correspondence or anything else of a personal nature.

There was nothing to see in the Canine Customers anteroom. I went from there through the foyer, into a sprawling living room.

Enough daylight filtered in past drawn blinds and shades to let me see without having to put on a light. A lot of money had been spent in furnishing it, but in a haphazard and tasteless way. Heavy antique tables and chairs of different styles, woods, and time periods, a glass-fronted cabinet crammed with gilt-patterned chinaware, heavy floor lamps with fringed crimson shades, an intricately patterned red and blue Oriental carpet that clashed with a couple of big, ugly modernistic paintings hung on two walls.

Here and there were empty spaces marked by dust lines where other, smaller pieces of furniture had stood. A section of a third wall above a secretary desk and next to a closed-off fireplace was bare except for a couple of metal brackets where something large and rectangular had been mounted; its faint outline was also visible when I got up close enough. One of those monster flat-screen TV sets, probably.

Too many items missing for them all to have been included with the boxes and other stuff Chavez had seen the two women loading into the SUV, so they must have been taken away on previous hauls. Told me two things: McManus and Carson had been planning to move out for at least a couple of days but weren't panicked enough to leave behind the bulk of their easily transportable possessions, and wherever they were hauling the stuff to, whether a permanent or an interim location, had to be relatively close to the city.

In the inner wall was an open doorway that led into a cluttered sitting room. Nothing for me there. And nothing in the kitchen and dining room except more residue of hasty and careless packing. Behind the kitchen at the back of the house was a smallish bedroom, comfortably but not as opulently furnished as the common rooms, with a connecting cubicle that contained a toilet, sink, and tiny stall shower. The room they rented out, likely. The double bed was made, everything clean and in its place, but the bureau and nightstand drawers, the closet, and the bathroom were empty. Nobody living here now. I wondered how long it had been vacant. There was a faint odor of cleaning fluid in the bathroom.

I went back the way I'd come, through the sitting room. Between the carpet there and the one in the living room was a section of hardwood floor. The floor had been waxed recently; I hadn't paid much attention the first time through, but this time the bottom of one shoe slid a little on the slick surface. That was what made me look down, then stop and look more closely.

There was enough light for me to make out a dark discoloration near the fringed edge of the living-room carpet. I dropped to one knee. Irregular stain like a Rorschach blot where something had seeped into the boards. An abortive effort had been made to scrub it away; you could see the marks left by a brush dipped in abrasive detergent.

Bloodstain?

I got out my penlight, shone the beam close above the stain. Might be blood, but I couldn't be sure. Couldn't be sure how long it had been there, either, though it didn't appear to be very old.

If it was blood, it hadn't come from a minor wound. A fair amount had leaked onto the floor to soak that deeply into the grain of the wood—the kind of seepage you get from direct or near direct contact with a surface. From a person dead or wounded, for instance, a person stabbed or shot or violently clubbed. Or attacked by a vicious dog.

I climbed the staircase to the second floor. The master bedroom had a massive four-poster bed that had the look of a Victorian antique; the rest of the furniture and adornments were the same expensive mismatches as those downstairs. Discarded articles of clothing were strewn over the bed, another garish Oriental carpet, the closet floor. Different sizes, different tastes as near as I could tell, indicating that McManus and Carson had shared this room. I quicksearched drawers and shelves. Nothing but minor leavings.

The medicine cabinet in the adjacent blue-tiled bathroom was open, the shelves mostly empty. Broken glass and spilled liquid from a dropped and broken bottle of nail polish marred the white porcelain sink; the splashes of polish were the color of fresh blood.

Across the hall were two more bedrooms, one of them made up but unused, the other turned into storage space, with another bathroom sandwiched between them. The storage room was a welter of empty, half-empty, and filled cartons. The contents of some had been upended and stirred through—clothing, odds and ends, a shiny scatter of costume jewelry. I opened two of the filled boxes: mustysmelling linens in one, articles of women's clothing in the second. The clothing was of different sizes and different styles and looked to be the sort elderly women would wear.

I dug down into a third box. A couple of dark suits, old but of quality manufacture, some ancient ties, and four white shirts still in their laundry wrappings—all of a size and a style that would belong to a tall, thin man who'd lived at least three-quarters of a century. And folded at the bottom was the clincher: a heavy, old-fashioned black overcoat with a velvet collar. I ran my fingers over the material. Soft wool. Lamb's wool. Gregory Pappas's coat.

There was no point in going through any of the other stuff; McManus and Carson had had plenty of time to sift out and pack up items of value and anything that might be incriminating. I'd been in the house too long, anyway. The place had begun to have an oppressive effect on me. I'd always been place sensitive, particularly to places where bad things had happened, and this one had that kind of aura about it, hardly noticeable when I'd first come in but now almost palpable.

The aura of evil.

19

ALEX CHAVEZ

The Explorer headed straight up Nineteenth and through Golden Gate Park on Park Presidio, riding the middle lane all the way. Definitely heading for the bridge. But why had McManus taken such a roundabout crosstown route? Quicker one to the bridge from Dogpatch was the 280 freeway into town, then out Geary to Park Presidio. She and Carson hadn't made any stops along the way, so that wasn't the answer. Maybe it was just that they preferred the longer route for some reason, weren't in a hurry to get to wherever they were going.

Getting on toward the start of rush hour and traffic through the park was stop-and-go; Chavez had to work to keep two to three cars behind them, changing back and forth between the middle and the far right lanes. A delivery truck cut in front of him in the Presidio tunnel, but he managed to maneuver around it just before the toll plaza.

When he first rolled onto the bridge, he didn't see the Explorer because of the great gouts of blanketing fog rolling in through the Gate, but he knew they hadn't gotten off at the last S.F. exit. A couple of quick weaving maneuvers through the clustered vehicles and he spotted them again—still in the middle lane, going the speed limit. He eased over into the same lane, slowing to match their speed, and stayed there three car lengths back.

How far up 101 were they going? Due north? East? You could get to Highway 80 by crossing the Richmond Bridge or taking 37 along the north shore of San Pablo Bay past Vallejo. Or some other direction or destination? Well, he'd find out. Tamara had told him to stay with the subjects as long and as far as he could.

He hoped it wouldn't be too long or too far, wouldn't require an overnight stay somewhere. The older he got, the less he liked being away from Elena and the kids for even one night. He'd have to call her pretty soon in any case, let her know he wouldn't be home for dinner. Some terrific woman, always worrying about him and his welfare. And the way she'd handled that tagging business with Tomas last week. Graffiti artist! Hah! The boy wanted to be an artist, fine, but spray-painting stupid symbols on public property wasn't an art project; it was a *crime*. Chavez had gone ballistic when he found out, but not Elena. Lectured and shamed Tomas, laid out a just-right punishment, and didn't raise her voice the entire time.

Better wait to call her until after he checked in again with Tamara. At least wait and see if McManus took the Richmond Bridge exit south of San Rafael.

Chavez glanced at the fuel gauge. Three-quarters full, good for maybe a hundred and fifty miles. If the subjects were going any farther than that, gas was liable to be a problem. But even if the Explorer's tank had been topped off when they left Dogpatch, the Explorer'd be near empty at about the same time as the Dodge—those big SUVs got lousy mileage—and with any luck he'd be able to pull off and fill up when they did.

Once they were off the bridge, traffic opened up a little. The Explorer moved over into the third of the four lanes; Chavez waited several seconds and then did the same. They wound up the long grade to the MacArthur Tunnel at fifty-five, passed through and down winding Waldo Grade on the Marin side. The fog was heavy here, too, streaming down from the cliffs in coils and stringy loops, laying a wet film on the windshield. Chavez switched on the wipers. The blades were new, but the windshield wasn't; he had to lean forward, squinting through the smeared glass.

They curled down to the foot of the grade, the SUV still in the third lane and moving at a steady fifty-five, Chavez two cars and not much more than a hundred yards behind. The highway sign for the Marin City exit swam up out of the mist. Once they passed it, not far ahead, the one for the Mill Valley–Stinson Beach exit appeared.

And all of a sudden, so unexpectedly it caught him and several other drivers by surprise, the pursuit ended.

Brake lights flashed and the SUV swerved dangerously into the far right lane, causing the driver of a pickup to brake hard, nearly fishtail. McManus kept on veering right, the bulky Explorer wobbling and sliding into the exit lane while the slow-lane traffic bunched up behind the pickup.

There was nothing Chavez could do, no way he could get over in time to make the exit himself.

"Maldito!"

The word exploded out of him with such ferocity that Elmo jumped up on the backseat and began a frightened yipping.

Long way to the next exit, across Richardson Bay. He drove as fast as he dared, turned off, and came back around southbound to the Mill Valley–Stinson Beach exit. The Mill Valley road was jammed with homeward-bound commuters; even if the Explorer was among all the tightly packed headlights and taillights, trying to locate it would be an exercise in futility. McManus also could have turned off on one of the side streets and doubled back onto the freeway northbound, or even southbound to return to the city. There was just no way to tell.

The woman must be plain crazy to have pulled that sudden lane change stunt on fog-slick pavement. Either that or she'd been alert to a tail and spotted him despite his precautions. Sure, that was it. Explained the roundabout crosstown route to the bridge.

Not his fault, then. You'd have to be invisible to follow somebody who's on the lookout for it. But that didn't make him feel any better.

All that mattered was, he'd lost them.

20

JAKE RUNYON

He had agency work to attend to after leaving Dragovich's office, in and out of the city; he spent four hours doing it, keeping his mind on a strict business focus the entire time. Continually agonizing about Bryn and her situation was wasted energy, negative energy.

The last piece of business was an interview in the Haight; from there he drove to the Hall of Justice. He hadn't heard from Dragovich, which likely meant that Bryn was still AdSeg'd. That was the case, dammit. He still couldn't get in to see her.

Three thirty-five. Twenty-five minutes to kill before the homicide inspectors, Farley and Crabtree, came on for their four-to-midnight tour. Runyon went into the cafeteria, bought himself a cup of tea and a corned-beef sandwich. He wasn't hungry, but he hadn't eaten all day and he needed to put something into his empty stomach.

At four o'clock he went up to General Works. Crabtree and Farley had both signed in, but neither was at his desk in the

Homicide Division. Runyon did some more waiting, nearly ten minutes, before Crabtree showed up carrying a sheaf of computer printouts.

"Your timing's good, Mr. Runyon. Just the man we wanted to see."

"If it's about my statement, that's one reason I'm here."

"It's about more than that. Mrs. Darby's statement, primarily."

"What about her statement?"

"It's full of lies."

Runyon felt himself tighten up inside. "What makes you think that?"

"Not think it, know it for a fact."

"How?"

Crabtree gestured to an empty chair, then leaned back and laced his fingers at the back of his neck. Big man, very dark, with a shaved head and, as if by way of compensation, a thick, bristly mustache. Neatly, almost nattily dressed in a brown pin-striped suit, salmon-colored shirt, brownish gold tie.

"Francine Whalen wasn't killed in a struggle with Mrs. Darby," he said. "Evidently wasn't killed by Mrs. Darby, in self-defense or otherwise. Preliminary lab tests are in. Three identifiable partials on the handle of the knife, another partial on the kitchen counter. None of them belong to her."

That was the last thing Runyon expected to hear. He digested the news before he asked, "Who do they belong to?"

"We don't know yet. Could be anybody's. Even yours."

"I never touched the knife. You think my story's a lie, too?"

"Is it? Any part of it?"

"No. All I know about what happened is what I told you

yesterday. So what now? Drop the homicide charge against Mrs. Darby, release her?"

"Depends on what she has to say to my partner. He's up talking to her right now. If she doesn't come clean, we'll keep right on holding her and let the DA decide. He may want to pursue an obstruction charge at her arraignment."

Runyon was silent.

"She's protecting somebody," Crabtree said. "That's pretty obvious. You were there—you're the logical first choice."

"And the wrong one. I had no reason to harm Francine Whalen."

"Who do you suppose it is, then?"

"I don't know."

But he did know. There was only one person Bryn would lie to protect, the most important person in her life.

Her son, Bobby.

Bobby. Nine years old, quiet, shy. Not a big kid, but wiry, strong. Capable of plunging a knife into the woman who'd been abusing him?

His Saturday wish that he had a gun like Runyon's to "keep for the next time" she hurt him . . . wishful thinking, a mistreated kid's fantasy, but maybe symptomatic of a genuine dark urge. Like the look on his face when he'd said, "I hate her, I hate her, *I hate her!*" just before jumping out of the car and running into the house. A boy his age might think about firing a handgun at an adult, but even if he had the opportunity he wasn't likely to go through with it unless he'd been taught how to use one, something Bryn would never have permitted. It took nerve, a steady hand, and a certain callousness to deliberately blow somebody away.

But it didn't take any of those things to make a killing thrust with a sharp kitchen knife. Self-defense weapon, the kind even a nine-year-old might snatch up if it was close at hand and he'd just been hurt again, was bleeding from a blow to the face and jammed up with fury, hate, humiliation. One quick blind jab, then the reactive shock when he realized what he'd done, and the guilt-ridden retreat within himself.

Was that the way it happened?

Bryn must think so. There was no other reason why she'd have taken the blame. It explained her sudden emotional shift: the immediate reaching out to the only man in her life she trusted, while still in a state of shock, then her protective maternal instincts taking over, calming her down so that she could fabricate her story; that was why the story had struck him as rehearsed. It also explained why she'd gone against his advice and volunteered information at the crime scene: trying to keep the focus on her. The other thing that had been bothering him was clear now, too—the words she'd been saying to Bobby in the boy's bedroom. *It's going to be all right, baby. It's going to be all right. You didn't do anything wrong, it was all just a bad dream. Don't think about it, forget it ever happened. It's going to be all right.* She hadn't only been reassuring her son; she'd also been absolving him and urging him to keep quiet.

But did she know for a fact that Bobby had done it? Had she found him in the kitchen with the body and his hands stained with Francine's blood, listened to him tell her he was responsible? Or was the boy already in shock and uncommunicative when she got there and she'd just assumed he'd done it because nobody else was in the flat? Could've happened that way, too. Bobby could be innocent. And if he was, then who was guilty?

Runyon didn't blame Bryn for trying to shield her son. Or for lying about it; she'd known he wouldn't go along with the cover-up. It was a relief to know that she hadn't had a direct hand in Whalen's death, but Christ, all she'd succeeded in doing was complicating an already-difficult situation, making things difficult for herself. A charge of obstruction wasn't nearly as serious as a homicide charge, but if she was prosecuted and convicted, she'd still face prison time.

All of this went through Runyon's mind while Crabtree put him through another ten minutes of Q & A, checking points in his statement, maybe looking in vain to trip him up. But he didn't confide any of it to the inspector. Let him and his partner figure it out on their own, if they didn't already suspect it.

Farley's appearance put an end to the questioning. The two inspectors left Runyon sitting there and went into a huddle nearby. When they came back, Farley—shorter, thinner, and lighter skinned than Crabtree, with drooping eyelids that gave him a deceptively sleepy look—confirmed what Runyon had expected: Bryn had denied she was covering for anybody, kept sticking to her story. Claimed no knowledge of whose prints were on the knife.

Crabtree said, "Maybe you can convince her to cooperate, Mr. Runyon. Want to give it a try?"

"Can I talk to her alone?"

"Along with her attorney, sure."

"I don't mean in an interrogation room with you listening behind glass. I mean just her and me, in private."

"You know we can't allow that while she's in AdSeg," Crabtree said.

Runyon knew it, but he had to ask. He didn't want to bring Bobby's name up to Bryn in front of an audience if there was a way around it. In order to get through to her, he had to know what she knew and was hiding about the murder. If she was certain Bobby was guilty, she'd never give him away.

"So what do you say, Mr. Runyon? Do it our way?"

"I doubt it'd do any good. If she was going to confide in me, she'd've done it at the crime scene."

"Maybe she did," Farley said mildly. "Maybe you're the one she's protecting."

Blowing smoke, the same as Crabtree had. They weren't all that suspicious of him—they'd have checked his record and found it clean—but they were good cops covering all the bases. He'd have handled it the same way when he carried a police badge.

He said, "You'll find out soon enough those prints on the knife aren't mine."

"So then you shouldn't mind helping us get to the bottom of this. Save Mrs. Darby a lot of trouble if you can convince her to open up. Are you willing to give it a try?"

"I'll have to talk to her attorney before I give you an answer."

"You want to call him now?"

"Yes. He hasn't been informed about the prints yet, has he?"

"Hasn't been time."

"I'll tell him, then."

Runyon went out into the hall to make the call. But Dragovich wasn't at his law office; his secretary said he'd

gone to a meeting on another case and that he wasn't scheduled back in today. Runyon tried the attorney's cell number.
Crap. Voice mail.

He went back into the Homicide Division. "Unavailable,"
he said to the inspectors.

"So the talk will have to wait," Farley said. "Just don't let
it wait too long."

"I won't."

"And don't let yourself become unavailable, meanwhile."

"I was on the job for fifteen years myself, remember? I
know the drill."

"Sure you do. But sometimes even ex-cops get careless."

"Only if they have a reason," Runyon said. "If you want
me before Dragovich or I get in touch, I'll be where you
can find me."

He was at loose ends, now. Nothing to do, nowhere to go,
until he heard from Dragovich. He'd promised Bryn he'd
try to find out how Bobby was doing, but there wasn't any
way to accomplish that short of asking the boy's father, and
Darby wouldn't be forthcoming. Dragovich might know;
she'd asked him to check as well. Again, nothing to do but
wait for the lawyer's return call.

The agency or his apartment? After five now and South
Park was closer to the Hall of Justice, but Tamara would
probably still be at the agency. She meant well, he was fond
of her, but she'd ask a lot of questions that he was in no
mood to answer. Home, then. If you could call a four-room,
cheaply furnished apartment home.

The drive up over Twin Peaks and down to Ortega took
nearly half an hour. Still no word from Dragovich by the time

Runyon got there. The apartment had a faintly musty odor he hadn't been aware of before: too long without an airing. He turned up the heat and then went to open the bedroom window partway, letting the chill evening breeze come swirling in.

On his way back past the bed, his gaze automatically went to the framed photograph of Colleen on the nightstand. He stopped for a few seconds to look at it. Not a day went by that he didn't think about her. But the thoughts were no longer morbid, heavy with the crippling grief that had obsessed him for so long; only sadness remained to darken the memories of their two decades together. Bryn was in his life now and he'd keep her in it no matter what happened with this Whalen crisis, but not as a replacement for Colleen. Different kind of relationship, different emotional needs. A mortal version of life after death.

He brewed himself a cup of tea. Some still edible cheese in the fridge and half a box of crackers, but the prospect of another small, tasteless meal like all those he prepared when he was alone made his stomach churn. In the living room he started to turn the television on, changed his mind, and left it dark. No stomach tonight, either, for the company of talking heads and flickering screen images.

He let himself go dark, too. Sat in his waiting mode on the couch, the tea untouched. He would have sat there like that for hours if he'd had to, but he didn't have to; it was no more than ten minutes before he finally heard from Dragovich.

Runyon ran down the latest developments for the lawyer, including his suspicion that the person Bryn was covering for was her son.

"Good news on the one hand," Dragovich said, "not so

good on the other. I can mount a strong argument at her arraignment that the homicide charge be dismissed for lack of
evidence, but the district attorney is likely to pursue an obstruction charge unless she recants her false story and admits
she's protecting her son. In that case, the judge will surely
rule in their favor. Most judges take a dim view of any de-
tained suspect who willfully makes a false statement that
hinders a police investigation, no matter what the reason."

"And if Bryn does recant and cooperate?"

"Then given the extenuating circumstances I doubt
there'll be any further charges. The judge might declare her
a material witness, but even if he should, she'd be released
from custody. But I gather from my face-to-faces with Mrs.
Darby, and from what you say, that convincing her won't
be easy."

"Not as long as she believes Bobby is guilty."

"Do you believe he is?"

"No, but it is possible. If I could talk to him . . . but I don't
suppose there's any way you can make that happen?"

"Not with Robert Darby in his present state of mind."

Runyon said, "What about me talking to Bryn without
the conversation being monitored? Or the three of us in private?"

"I'll talk to Farley and Crabtree, but they have every reason to stand on protocol. If you're allowed to see her, I'm
afraid it will have to be with an official audience. Of course,
I can consult with her alone and try to persuade her."

"No offense, but I stand a better chance of getting through
to her and finding out what she knows. How soon can you
arrange the meeting?"

"Tonight, if they're agreeable."

. . .

Runyon brewed another cup of tea while he waited for Dragovich to call back. Too strong, bitter; he dumped it out. For the first time in a long time, since the rock-bottom night shortly after Colleen's death when he'd sat with a bottle of bourbon in one hand and his .357 Magnum in the other, he felt like having a drink of hard liquor. There was none in the apartment, but even if there had been, he wouldn't have given in to the momentary craving. He'd never been much of a drinking man, and Angela's alcoholism and his near suicide had turned him dry except for an occasional beer. Booze for a man like him was a problem, not a problem solver.

It was fifteen minutes before his cell vibrated again. And only the first part of what Dragovich had to tell him was what he wanted to hear.

"Preliminary reports on the fingerprints have come in," the attorney said. "You're off the hook and so is Robert Darby."

"ID match?"

"None yet. It's possible whoever wielded the knife was never fingerprinted. They're still checking."

So it could still be Bobby. Wasn't likely Darby would've consented to the boy being printed, even if Crabtree and Farley had thought to suggest it; later, if it became necessary to Bryn's defense, Dragovich could get a court order to compel the father to allow it. The fact that a child's fingers were small didn't necessarily mean anything, either. Plenty of adults had hands and fingers not much larger than a nine-year-old's. You could get an ID match from bloody partials, but without a full clear latent and a comparison source, the lab techs would make the same assumption as the investigating officers: the prints belonged to an adult.

Runyon asked, "When do we get to talk to Bryn?"

"The best I could do is tomorrow morning at nine o'clock."

Damn. "Delaying tactic?"

"Partly. If I know the DA, his intention is to keep her segregated to give her time to think over her position now that she's been caught in her lie. He also wants an ADA present during the interview. Neither his office nor the police are in any hurry—there are still forty-eight hours left before Mrs. Darby is scheduled for arraignment. I suggest you and I meet beforehand for a strategy conference. Eight thirty in the community room, third floor at Eight-fifty Bryant?"

"I'll be there."

"Is there anything else we need to discuss tonight?"

"Bryn's son. I don't suppose Darby returned your call?"

"He did, as a matter of fact. Professional courtesy."

"How's the boy?"

"Well enough physically, but he still won't talk about the alleged abuse or what, if anything, he may know about Francine Whalen's death."

"Who's taking care of him?"

"A nurse Darby hired. He seems to be in good hands."

No, he wasn't. Runyon found that out twenty minutes later.

When the doorbell rang, he almost didn't answer it. The only people who came around while he was home were solicitors and, once, one of his neighbors looking to borrow something. But the bell kept up an insistent ringing, and when

Runyon finally responded he found himself face-to-face with Robert Darby. A distraught and angry Robert Darby.

"Have you seen him?" Darby said. "Is he here with you?"

"Who? You don't mean Bobby—"

"Damn right I mean Bobby. He ran away this afternoon and I've looked everywhere else. If you're hiding him, Runyon, I swear to God I'll make you wish you were never born."

21

Tamara was beside herself over what she called "those two bitches' escape." Not that she blamed Alex Chavez for the lost tail. He was an experienced field man and he'd taken every precaution, but no op can maintain road surveillance when he's been spotted and the subjects are bent on ditching him. The dangerous last-second lane change would have caught anybody in the profession by surprise.

Alex felt bad about it, though. He'd driven straight back to Dogpatch to stake out the 20th Street house in case McManus and Carson decided to go back there. Chances of that happening were nil now, but Alex had insisted. And Tamara and I both knew his professional ethics wouldn't allow him to take any overtime pay for the extended stakeout, either.

What upset and frustrated her—me, too—was that we were still hamstrung by the lack of hard evidence necessary to convince the law to take immediate action. What I'd found in the house was plenty suspicious, but we couldn't report it without admitting that I'd been guilty of illegal trespass and unlawful entry, and my uncorroborated testimony alone wouldn't constitute sufficient cause for a judge to issue a search

warrant. Cops and judges frown on private investigators sub-
verting the law in any way. So does the state Board of Licenses.
And never mind the rationale.

By the time I got back to the office, Tamara had used the
information The Dog Hole barfly Frank Quarles had given
me to run a deep backgrounder on Gregory Pappas. The name
wasn't all that uncommon, but she was sure she had the right
man. Born in Athens, Greece, in 1929, immigrated to the
U.S. in 1946. Worked for a San Francisco relative who owned
a Greek restaurant. Opened his own place on Polk Street, the
Acropolis Restaurant, in 1959 and operated it until 1992,
when it was gutted by an accidental grease fire. Underin-
sured, so he hadn't been able to rebuild or reopen elsewhere—
but he'd gotten enough of a settlement, and apparently had
had enough put away, to live comfortably in retirement. Married, no children. Wife deceased in 1998. Never owned a
home; lifelong apartment dweller. After his wife's death,
moved from the apartment he'd shared with her in the Anza
Vista neighborhood to a smaller apartment in the Potrero.
Lived at that address for a dozen years until the building was
sold and went condo. Residence after that presumably the
house in Dogpatch, but nothing to confirm it. Present whereabouts unknown. And most significantly, no death record
anywhere.

"They killed him," Tamara said. "McManus and Carson.
Just like they killed Rose O'Day and Virden and God knows
how many others."

"Murder for profit."

"Murder *factory*. Rent that room to somebody with no
close friends or relatives, somebody with money or other
valuables. Victim doesn't come to them soon enough, one or

both of 'em go trolling for one in Mission Bay or SoMa or Potrero Hill. That's how they found Rose O'Day, right?"

"According to Selma Hightower."

"Then when they got everything they could from those poor old folks, they offed 'em. Probably been doing it the whole seven years they lived there."

"The real Roxanne McManus doesn't fit that victim profile," I pointed out.

"Maybe she was how they got started, part of Mama Psycho's plan to set up the dog-boarding front."

"Here's another possibility," I said. "Mama Psycho, as you call her, needed a new identity because she has a criminal record somewhere. Might even be a fugitive warrant out on her."

"Carson, too, I'll bet. Thelma and Louise."

"Who?"

"That's right, the only flicks you watch are old black-and-whites on TV."

"What do movies have to do with this?"

"Never mind," she said. "So McManus and Carson are running this murder factory, nobody suspects anything for seven years, and then along come Virden and us investigating and they can see the whole thing starting to unravel. Virden thinks things over in The Dog Hole after his first visit to the house and decides maybe we didn't screw up after all. Goes back to confront the impostor, threatens to go to the cops— and that's the end of him."

I agreed that that was a likely enough scenario, given the bloodstain I'd found in the living room.

"We keep investigating," Tamara said, "and McManus tries to warn you off with the lawsuit threat. Smoke screen to buy them time—they've already decided to haul ass out of Dodge. We're getting too close to the truth and they can't afford to wait around. So they empty their bank accounts, dig up their cash stash, whatever, and start loading up their SUV. Man, I wish we had some idea where they took all that stuff of theirs."

"Storage unit somewhere, maybe."

"Come back for it later, after things've cooled down? That'd be pretty risky. Seems more likely they'd want to get far away from San Francisco and never come back."

"Depends on what their plans are. They're too shrewd to run blind—they'd have a hideout set up or in mind."

"So they could be anywhere now."

"Just about. One thing they'll do before they go very far is switch that SUV for another set of wheels, make themselves even harder to trace."

"We can't just sit back and let them get away," Tamara said grimly. "We've got to do *something*."

I said, "I've already told the SPCA about the abandoned dogs. And I've got a call in to Jack Logan. When I hear from him, I'll lay out everything we suspect. He knows I wouldn't come to him unless I was reasonably sure I had good cause."

"But will he do anything even if you fess up to unlawful entry?"

"Whatever he can. The abandoned dogs should give the police the right to inspect the kennels. McManus's and Carson's prints are bound to be in there, and if we're right that the two of them are fugitives, that'll be enough cause for a search warrant for the house."

"All that's gonna take a long time," Tamara said. "Too long."

"No use worrying about what we can't control. Even if APBs were put out right away, it might already be too late. They could already be off the highways by now, holed up someplace."

"Yeah."

"Look at it this way," I said. "No matter what happens, they won't be killing any more people in Dogpatch."

"I'd feel better about that if I knew they won't be killing any more people anywhere." She was silent for several seconds. Then, "I keep wondering what happened to the bodies. No place on the property where they could've buried 'em?"

"Not unless there's a pit hidden under the kennels."

". . . You think maybe?"

"No, I don't. Chancy disposal method anyway."

"What about that sick dude in Ohio a couple of years ago, had decomposing and mummified corpses all over his house and yard?"

"Different type of case. Trust me—there aren't any corpses hidden on the Dogpatch property."

"So maybe they cut 'em up and fed 'em to the dogs."

"Pretty grisly work for a couple of middle-aged women."

"Well? Men don't have a monopoly on being monsters."

She was right enough about that. But whatever the answer, I had a feeling it wasn't chopped-up human dog food.

Jack Logan hadn't returned my call by the time I headed home. I'd left two messages for him, one on his cell's voice mail, the other at the Hall of Justice, both stressing the urgency of the information I had for him, but he'd become a busy man since his promotion to assistant chief. The constant demands on his time came not only from the PD but also from the city's political hierarchy and individuals a lot more powerful and influential than I would ever be. Jack and I had been friends a long time, but that didn't count for much on the priority ladder.

In the old days I'd had other friends in the department I could have appealed to, but they were all gone now—retired, working for other police departments or at other jobs. One more example of the effects of time erosion. There were a few inspectors I'd had business dealings with, but I didn't know any of them well enough to approach them with a handful of nothing much more than speculation based on circumstantial evidence. Logan was the only one who'd give Tamara's and my suspicions the attention they deserved.

Mild argument with Kerry when I got home. She wanted to go out to dinner—Emily was spending the night with a friend—and I wanted to stay in, relax after the long day, wait for Logan's call. She won the argument, as she usually does when she really wants something, by a combination of cajolery, guilt-tripping (we hadn't been out together alone in weeks), and subtle sexual promise. Not that she used sex the way some women did, as a form of extortion. She'd never said no to me just because she didn't get her way—too honest and caring for that kind of nonsense. But if she did get her way, her natural tendency was to be more enthusiastic in her lovemaking. I may be crowding geezerhood, but I can still be as swayed by the prospect of enthusiasm as I was in my younger days.

So we went out to dinner, at a Sicilian restaurant that had just opened up in Noe Valley. My one proviso being that I keep my cell phone on because Logan still hadn't rung back.

Normally doing that goes against my grain—people who get calls and then chatter in public places are near the top of my list of my pet peeves—but this was a special circumstance. Kerry had no objection when I explained the situation on the drive down to 24th Street.

The restaurant was crowded; we had to wait twenty minutes for a table. Worth the wait: the food and the service were both first-rate. I had chicken marsala, Kerry a pasta dish called *finocchio con sarde,* made with fennel and sardines, that tasted a whole lot better than it sounds, and we shared a bottle of light Corinto wine. The place was atmospherically decorated and the lighting kept purposely dim in order to maximize the effect of candlelight. Kerry looks good in any light, the more so since she'd treated herself (and me) to the facelift after her bout with breast cancer, but there's something about candle glow that makes her especially attractive. Gives her auburn hair a kind of fiery shine, her face a luminous, ageless quality. The longer I looked at her across the table, the more glad I was that I'd lost the argument tonight. Enthusiasm. Right. I could feel mine rising by the minute.

We were sipping the last of our wine when she broke a brief conversational lull by saying, "Tom Bates just bought a second home, a small ranch down in the Carmel Valley."

"Good for him. He can afford it."

"We could afford one, too, you know."

"What, in Carmel Valley? I don't think so."

"No, you're right; the Carmel area is too expensive. But somewhere else—Lake County, the Sierras, the north coast."

"You're not serious about this?"

"Why not? Wouldn't you like to have a weekend getaway place?"

"I don't know . . . would you?"

"Yes. I love the city as much as you do, but a change of scenery now and then would be good for both of us. Emily, too. I don't mean day trips—quiet weekends, minivacations."

"You sure we can afford it?" Kerry handled all the household financial matters; she has a much better head for figures than I do.

"Since Jim Carpenter promoted me to vice president we can. The market's down now; we could get a small cabin or cottage for a reasonable price." The prospect excited her; the candlelight emphasized the high color in her cheeks. "And we could take our time looking in different areas until we find just the right place. It'd be fun."

"You really think we'd use a second home enough to make it worthwhile? I mean, we don't get away on weekend trips much as it is."

"That's just the point," she said. "We wouldn't keep finding excuses to stay home or take only short day trips if we had a place of our own to go to. You're supposed to be semi-retired, but you're right back to working four and five days a week. Wouldn't you like to take more time off, do something besides sit around the condo when you're not at the agency?"

"You work longer hours than I do."

"Yes, and I'd like to cut back a little myself eventually. Don't you think we're entitled to some leisure time? We're not exactly spring chickens, you know."

"Don't need to remind me."

"There are other benefits, too," she said. "Buying a piece of California real estate is always a good investment, no matter where it is, and it'll help our tax situation. And you know we're almost out of storage space at the condo. We could move a lot of stuff to a getaway place, not just nonessentials but utilitarian items like clothes and furniture. The living-room couch, for instance. I'd been wanting to buy a new— What's the matter? Why are you staring off like that?"

"Storage space," I said.

". . . What about it?"

"Piece of California real estate. Storage space."

"Are you all right? You have the oddest look on your face—"

"Lightbulb just went off." I slid my chair back. "Wait here; finish your wine. I'll be right back."

"Where're you going?"

"Make a phone call to Tamara."

I tried her home number first; it was late enough so that she should be there by now. Five rings, while I stood shivering on the sidewalk in front of the restaurant. On the sixth ring, she answered sounding grumpy.

"Got me out of the tub," she said. "What's up?"

"That piece of rural property Rose O'Day inherited. Didn't you say it was in Marin County?"

"Some place called the Chileno Valley."

"What kind of property? How big?"

"Farmland. Thirty acres."

"Buildings on it?"

"I'd have to check the tax records, but—" She broke off and then let out a little yip; quick on the uptake, as always. "And the Chileno Valley is west of Highway One-oh-one go-ing north. That's where McManus and Carson were headed— *that's* where they're hiding out!"

22

JAKE RUNYON

Robert Darby cooled down some after Runyon let him come in and look through the apartment. Darby stood flushed and jittery in the middle of the living room, his red-eyed gaze flicking here and there without resting on Runyon or anything else for more than a second. Man badly in need of rest, beset by grief, anxiety, impotent rage. An unlikable, self-centered shyster whose treatment of Bryn was little short of cruel, but seeing him like this, you couldn't help but feel for him.

"You're sure you haven't seen Bobby, heard from him?"

Second time Darby had asked that question. Runyon gave him a slightly different version of the same answer. "I'd tell you if I had. I'm not your enemy, Mr. Darby."

"All right. All right."

Runyon asked, "Did something happen to make the boy run away?"

"No." Darby shook his head, scraped fingernails through his close-cropped hair. "I don't understand it," he said. "The nurse I hired, she went in to use the bathroom and when she came out he was gone. Just like that . . . gone."

"How long ago?"

"A couple of hours. Just before I got home."

"No prior indication that's what he had in mind?"

"Didn't say a word to her. To me, either. Closed up tight since that horror show yesterday, wouldn't talk, wouldn't eat . . . ah, Christ. Where would he go?"

Runyon said, "His mother's house, maybe."

"No, he's not there; I just came from there. First place I thought of."

"Did you or the nurse tell him where Bryn's being held?"

". . . You think he went to the Hall of Justice?"

"Might have, if he has an idea that's where she is. You notify the police that he's missing?"

"No, I drove straight out here—"

Darby broke off, jerked his cell phone out of his coat pocket; fumbled it, almost dropped it in his haste. It took him a nervous two minutes to get through to either Farley or Crabtree; his voice rose and cracked a little as he talked. From Darby's end of the conversation Runyon gathered the boy hadn't been seen at the Hall and that they'd put out a BOLO alert for him.

"I should've called them sooner," Darby said when he ended the conversation. "First Francine, now this with Bobby . . . just not thinking straight."

"The police will find him. Best thing you can do is go home and wait for word."

"Don't tell me what to do, goddamn you!"

Runyon sidestepped the flare-up with a question. "Did Bobby take anything with him when he left? A bag, clothing?"

"What? No. The nurse looked, I looked . . . a jacket, that's all."

"What about money? Bus fare, cab fare."

"He couldn't have much, no more than a few dollars from his allowance. . . ." Darby shook himself, a sharp rippling action like a dog shaking off water. "What the hell am I doing standing here talking to you? If Bobby does come here or you hear from him, notify me right away. Understand?"

Runyon said, "You and the police both," but Darby was already on his way out.

Why had Bobby run away?

Bad environment in that flat, whether the boy had had anything to do with Whalen's death or not. Painful memories, ghosts haunting his impressionable mind. Fear made worse by his overbearing father's anger and grief, by a stranger called in to watch over him, by not being told what had happened to his mother. Sensitive, damaged kid huddled inside himself for security and solace, but too bright and too needy to stay that way for long. Perfectly natural that when he freed himself from his shell he'd want to free himself from his oppressive surroundings as well.

Where would he go?

Linked answer: familiar place where he felt safe, where he might find genuine comfort, where he might find his mother. Her house, his second home, the only real home he'd ever known—that was the logical choice.

Three hours. More than twice as much time as it would usually take to travel by bus from the Marina to the Sunset District. Unless he'd gotten lost or something had happened to him on the way . . . No, the hell with that kind of thinking.

But Darby had been to Bryn's house, presumably still had a key and searched it, and Bobby wasn't there—

Or was he?

The brown-shingled house was completely dark, sheathed in mist, when Runyon pulled up in front. Fast walk up the path and stairs to the front porch. Bryn kept a spare key in a little box mounted under the window ledge to the right of the door. He went there first, felt inside the box. Empty.

All right.

He had his own key to the place, as Bryn had one to his apartment—an in-case-of-emergency exchange and a measure of their mutual trust. He let himself in, closed the door behind him, and stood listening before he switched on the hall light. Silence except for the faint snaps and creaks you always heard in an old house in cold weather. Cold in there, too, with the furnace off or turned down; he could see the faint vapor of his breath as he made his way to the bedrooms at the rear.

Bobby's room was empty, the bed neatly made, everything in place. Same in Bryn's room. The spare bedroom, her office, the living room, the kitchen were just as empty. She kept a flashlight in the pantry; Runyon found it, tested it, and then opened the door to the basement and flicked on the light.

A short flight of stairs led downward. He hadn't been in the basement before, took a moment to orient himself. Furnace and water heater at the far wall. To his left, washer and dryer and storage cabinets; to his right, a workbench and rows of hand tools hung on a pegboard. Behind the water heater, Bryn had said. He crossed to it, found the narrow space where he could wedge his body behind the unit. The opening to the crawlspace that led deeper under the house was closed off by a sliding panel. He eased it open partway.

"Bobby? It's Jake."

Silence.

He slid the panel open the rest of the way. The pale overhead light didn't reach this far; all he could see inside was heavy blackness.

"It's okay for you to come out now," he said, keeping his voice low pitched, normal. "Your dad's gone. There's nobody here but me."

Silence.

"You can trust me, Bobby, you know that. I'm your friend and your mom's friend. I know where she is and I'm doing everything I can to help her. But I need you to help me do that."

Silence.

Runyon hesitated. He didn't want to go into the crawlspace himself or use the flashlight, but he had to be sure the boy was there. Had to get him out if he was, and without scaring him any more than he already was.

"I'm going to put on a light," Runyon said. "Don't be afraid. I just want to see where you are."

Faint rustling sound . . . the boy moving away from him? He leaned down to put his head and arm inside the musty opening, aimed the flash at an angle to one side, and flicked the switch.

Bare boards, disturbed dust, tattered spiderwebs jumped into sharp relief. Sounds of movement again in the deeper blackness beyond the reach of the light. He moved the beam along the side wall, not too fast, until it touched the crouched shape far back against a maze of copper piping. Bobby, one hand lifted to shield his eyes against the glare.

Immediately Runyon shut off the flash. "Okay, son," he said into the darkness. "Now that I know you're there, I'm going to go over and sit on the steps. Come on out when you're ready and we'll talk."

No response.

Runyon backed out of the opening, straightened to step around the water heater, then crossed to the stairs. He sat on the third riser from the bottom, the flashlight beside him, and waited.

Five minutes. Six, seven. If the boy didn't come out, Runyon wasn't sure what he'd do. Go in after him, carry him out? Not a good option, because it would likely damage what trust Bobby had in him, keep him withdrawn and silent. Leave him in there, call his father and the police? That wasn't much good, either. Finding out what the boy knew was imperative, and Runyon would never have a better opportunity than this.

Ten minutes. Eleven—

Faint scraping sounds from across the basement. A soft thud, as of a sneakered foot thumping against wood. A muffled cough. Coming out.

A few more seconds and the pale oval of Bobby's face peered around the edge of the water heater. Runyon didn't move, didn't say anything. Ten-second impasse. Then Bobby moved again, out into the open in slow, shuffling steps, blinking in the ceiling light.

He stopped in the middle of the basement, fifteen feet from where Runyon sat. Stood there in an attitude of expectant punishment, chin down, eyes rolled up under the thin blinking lids, shivering a little from the cold. A purplish bruise under his left eye, the aftereffect of Whalen's blow to his nose, showed starkly against the facial pallor. Web shreds clung to his hair; his light jacket and Levi's were streaked with dust and dirt smudges.

Looking at him, Runyon felt a long-forgotten emotion—a tenderness, an aching compassion that had its roots in fatherhood. The time Joshua had fallen out of his crib when he was a baby, bruising an arm . . . that was the last time Runyon had experienced that kind of feeling. As if this kid, this relative stranger, were his child. He had to stop himself from going to Bobby, wrapping him in a protective embrace.

"You don't have to be afraid of me, son," he said. "I won't hurt you. Nobody's ever going to hurt you again."

Four-beat. Then, in a scared little voice, "Where's my mom?"

"Don't worry, she's all right."

"Where is she? Why isn't she home?"

"It's cold down here," Runyon said. "Let's go upstairs and I'll put the furnace on. We'll talk up there."

No response.

He got to his feet in slow segments. Bobby watched him without moving. Runyon smiled at him, then pivoted and mounted the steps into the kitchen, leaving the door wide open. The thermostat was in the front hall; he went there and turned the dial up past seventy to get the heat flowing quickly. When he returned to the kitchen, the boy was standing in the basement doorway. So far so good.

Runyon said, keeping his distance, "It'll take a few minutes for the house to warm up. Want me to get you a blanket meanwhile?"

"No. Where's my mom?"

"I won't lie to you, Bobby. The police are holding her in jail."

"Jail? Why? She didn't do anything."

"I know that. The police will, too, before long."

"When will they let her come home? When can I see her?"

"Soon. Maybe tomorrow."

Some of the boy's tension seemed to ease, make him less skittish. His breathing was audible: little nasal hissing sounds.

Runyon said, "But there are some things I have to know in order for your mom to be released. About what happened yesterday."

No response.

"It's very important. I need you to talk to me about it, Bobby. For your mom's sake. Okay?"

Six-beat. Then, "Okay."

"You know Francine is dead?"

"Yes. I know."

"The police arrested your mom because they thought she killed Francine—"

"No! She didn't, it wasn't Mom."

"Who was it? Do you know?"

"Mom wasn't there; she came after."

"After Francine was killed?"

"Yes."

"How long afterward?"

"I don't know . . . a few minutes."

"Who was in the kitchen with Francine, Bobby?"

Headshake.

With the basement door still open, snapping, thrumming sounds from the cranked-up furnace were audible below. Reliable and efficient, that furnace, only a few years old; Bryn had told him that. Warm air pumping up through the heat registers had already begun to take the edge off the house's chill. Runyon moved to his left, then forward a little; Bobby responded as he'd intended, coming out of the doorway and sideways in the other direction, nearer the heat register.

"Somebody else was with Francine before your mom came, right?"

"Yes."

"Do you know who it was?"

"No."

"Man or woman?"

"I don't know. I didn't see."

"Couldn't hear them talking?"

"Just Francine. She . . . started yelling loud and weird. . . ."

"How do you mean, weird?"

"Stuff about cows."

"Cows?"

"That's what it sounded like. She said the ƒ word, too."

"How long was it after she hit you before the other person got there?"

Headshake.

"Bobby, we all know Francine was hurting you. Your mom said she hit you in the face, cut your cheek, and made your nose bleed. That's right, isn't it?"

". . . Yes."

"Why did she do it?"

"I wanted a snack, that's all. But she was taking a tray out of the oven and I got in her way and she burned herself." Bobby's face scrunched up at the memory; he pawed at it angrily, as if trying to rearrange it—as if trying to stop himself from crying.

"What did she say after she hit you?"

"Go wash the blood off, change my shirt. And tell my dad I fell down or she'd hurt me real bad. I hated her!"

"Enough to hurt her back?"

"I wanted to."

"But you didn't."

"No."

"Okay. So then you went to the bathroom—"

"No. Just to my room."

"Didn't wash off the blood or change your shirt?"

"I didn't feel good, I wanted to lie down."

"How long were you in your room before the other person came?"

"Not long. Couple of minutes, I guess."

"And you were still lying down when Francine started talking loud about cows and using the *f* word?"

"Yes."

"Can you remember anything else she said?"

"No. Just yelling and then a crash and . . . hitting sounds. Then she screamed, real loud and short."

Hitting sounds—Francine and her killer struggling, fighting. The scream from her as she was attacked with the knife, cut off short when the blade went into her chest.

Runyon asked, "What made the crash you heard?"

"Something breaking."

"In the kitchen?"

"I guess so."

"Do you know what it was?"

"No."

Something breaking in the kitchen, just as the struggle started. But there hadn't been any sign of breakage when Runyon had gone in there. His focus had been on the dead woman, but he'd never yet walked into a crime scene without his trained eye registering anything out of place, everything large enough to see. If there'd been glass or other shards on the floor, the countertops, in the sink, he'd have noticed. Yet Bobby had no reason to lie about hearing a crash. . . .

Runyon asked, "Did you stay in your room after you heard Francine scream?"

"Yes."

"For how long?"

"Until the door slammed. The front door."

"Did you go into the kitchen then?"

Nod. "Francine . . . she was lying there with blood all over. . . ." This time the memory made Bobby shudder. "I was *glad* she was dead. But it made me sick, too, and scared."

"Like you were having a bad dream."

"Yeah. I didn't know what to do."

"And that's when your mom came."

"Yes."

"Did you tell her you were glad Francine was dead?"

". . . I don't remember."

"But you told her everything you just told me—about the other person who was there."

Nod. "She made me change my clothes and lie down again with a wet towel on my nose. After that . . . I don't know, she acted funny. She kept saying don't tell Dad or anybody else what happened, don't say anything, she'd make everything all right."

Easy enough now to piece the rest of it together. Bryn may

or may not have believed Bobby's story at first, but with no evidence that anyone else had been in the flat to support it and her son's face and clothing still bloody, she'd mistakenly assumed the worst: Bobby hated Francine enough to want her dead; he'd retaliated for the blow in the face by stabbing her; some of the blood on his clothes was hers; he'd made up the story about another visitor out of guilt and fear. That was when Bryn decided to take the blame and try to keep the boy hushed up.

"Jake?"

"Yes, son?"

"Can I stay here until Mom comes home?"

Before he answered, Runyon went over to close the basement door. "I wish you could, but I think you know it's not possible."

"Why not? You don't have to tell my dad you found me."

"Yes, I do. The police, too—he's already told them you ran away."

"You said I could trust you. You said you're my friend."

"You can and I am. I only want what's best for you and your mom."

"Then let me stay here. Please." The boy's hands were tightly fisted now; his gaze skittered around the kitchen as if he were looking for a path of escape. "I don't want to go back to my dad's. I don't want to live there anymore; I want to live here with Mom."

"Maybe we can work that out. I'll talk to your mom's lawyer about it."

"Honest?"

"Yes. Promise. But you can't stay here now, not yet."

"Why can't I?"

"You can't keep on hiding, Bobby. Your dad's worried about you."

"I don't care."

"Yes, you do. You know he's hurting—you don't want to cause him any more pain, do you?"

". . . No."

"And you don't want me to get in trouble, right? Remember, I'm a detective. That means I have an obligation to obey the law, and the law says I have to take you back to your dad and notify the police that you're safe. If I don't, then I'll get in trouble and I won't be able to help bring your mom home. You understand?"

The boy's hands slowly unclenched; his gaze steadied again. And after a few seconds he murmured, "Yes."

"Okay. Tell you what. You must be hungry and so am I. Sit down and I'll fix us a couple of sandwiches before we leave."

No response. But when Runyon opened the fridge, Bobby moved over to sit at the dinette table and watch with moist, solemn eyes while he made the sandwiches.

23

Alex Chavez and I left the city in my car shortly past eight Saturday morning. He'd been more than agreeable to coming with me and had offered to do the driving, but it was my case and my decision to make this scouting expedition. I would've liked to bring Jake Runyon along, too, just in case, but he was so jammed up with the Bryn Darby matter I wouldn't have felt right pulling him away from it.

Traffic was light once we got across the Golden Gate Bridge; the thirty-mile ride to Novato in northern Marin, where we turned off, took not much more than half an hour. The sun was out for the first time in more than a week, with just a few streaky clouds and a light breeze. Nice day for a drive under different circumstances. Chavez is that rarity, a genuinely happy man, but he didn't have much to say today; he was still upset at himself for losing the McManus tail yesterday. I didn't feel much like conversation, either. We'd done all the talking necessary when I phoned him the night before to set this up.

One of my recent birthday presents from Kerry was a GPS unit—part of her ongoing and none-too-subtle efforts to drag me deeper into the techno age. I hadn't used the GPS much—I can't get used to the idea of a disembodied voice telling me to turn left, turn right, go straight for x number of miles as if I were a dunce who couldn't figure out the simple basics of getting from point A to point B. But I had to admit that the thing came in handy once you were off the beaten track and hunting a rural address in unfamiliar territory.

The Chileno Valley was several miles west and north of Novato, long and narrow and running through both Marin and Sonoma counties. Undeveloped countryside, of the sort that surprises visitors from other parts of the country who think California is all sprawling cities and suburbs, congested freeways, surfing beaches, wineries and vineyards, and tall mountains. A vast percentage of the state is still open space: desert, forests, farmland, pastureland, rolling hills and valleys that extend for miles. This valley was hemmed in by rounded winter green hills, some bare sided, others coated with live oaks and madrone. Long stands of eucalyptus bordered sections of the winding two-lane road that ran through it. Dairy cattle and occasional horses grazed in meadows and hollows. Farms and small ranches dotted the area, but they were few and generally far between.

The GPS gadget took us to the general vicinity of the number we were looking for, 8790, but neither Chavez nor I spotted it on the first pass. I had to turn around at the next address to the north, drive back at a reduced speed. No wonder we'd missed it: rusted tubular metal gate closed across a barely discernible dirt track, the number hand-painted on a drunken-leaning square of wood wired to the gate and so faded you couldn't read it clearly from more than a few feet away. The track snaked around a small tangled copse of oak, madrone, and pepper trees and disappeared through a declivity where a pair of hillsides folded down close together. According to the property records Tamara had checked, there were three buildings on Rose O'Day's thirty acres, but none of them was visible from anywhere on Chileno Valley Road.

Chavez said, "What now?"

"We'll have to go in, at least far enough to get a look at the place."

"On foot?"

"On foot."

"Okay with me." He flashed one of his infectious grins. "Be the first time I've trespassed on private property since I left the Imperial sheriff's department."

"I wish I could say the same."

I pulled ahead a hundred yards or so, to where the road curved to the left and there was a wide spot next to a small creek. Safe enough place to leave the car; there was little traffic on the road this morning and nobody passing by was likely to wonder why it was parked there.

Before we got out I reached into the backseat for the pair of Zeiss field glasses I'd moved in from the trunk earlier. Then I unclipped the emergency .38 Colt Bodyguard I keep under the dash, flipped the gate open to check the loads, put a cartridge under the hammer, and slid the piece into my jacket pocket. Chavez was armed as well; I'd asked him to bring his weapon. Technically we had no right to take handguns onto private property, but there was no way either of us was going into unfamiliar territory on business like this without protection. McManus and Carson were reason enough, if they were here and if we were right about them, but it was that yellow-eyed Rottweiler that worried me the most.

We walked back along the road to the gate. The morning was cold, windless, but there were breaks in the cloud cover that indicated a partial clearing later on. It was as if we had this part of the valley to ourselves—quiet except for birdsong, no cars passing, not even a cow in sight. A rusted chain and padlock held the gate fastened to a stanchion. I lifted the lock to peer at the key slot on its bottom.

"Scratches," I said. "Fairly fresh."

"So they're here."

"Or been and gone. We'll take it slow and careful."

A sagging barbed-wire fence stretched away on both sides of the gate, so we had to climb over. Chavez is short and stocky and looks plodding, but he moves with a smooth muscular agility when he needs to; he went up on one of the rails and over and down all in one motion. It took a little more effort for me to get up astride the top bar, but I scrambled down quick when I heard the sound of an approaching vehicle. We ducked in among the spicy-scented pepper trees before it came into sight. Pickup towing a horse trailer. The driver didn't even glance in our direction as he clattered by.

I led the way along the track, around the section of trees and underbrush to where we could see ahead to where it staggered in between the two hill folds. Still no buildings in sight. As much of the terrain as was visible beyond the declivity was open meadowland, the only ground cover at a distance. The track appeared to veer off to the right behind the bigger of the two hillsides; that must be where the buildings were.

Chavez figured it the same way. He said, "No telling how close the buildings are behind that hill. Want to risk staying on the road?"

"Not if we can help it. It's pretty open up there; I don't like the idea of walking in blind."

He gestured at the hillside on our left. "Might be able to get a view of the layout from up there."

I gave the hill a quick scan. It rose in a series of wrinkled creases to a height of a couple of hundred feet. Scrub oak and live oak and mossy juts of rock spotted it, a few of the lower trees little more than gray skeletons—victims of Sudden Oak Death. The ascent looked to be gradual; it ought to be easy enough to climb if we were careful and didn't rush it.

"Might as well give it a shot."

We backtracked a short ways until we found a place to start the climb. I let Chavez take the lead; he had twenty years on me, was in better condition, and had more stamina. Better trailblazing instincts, too, as it turned out. He picked the shortest and safest, if not always the most direct, route around the outcroppings and through the trees. And set a steady, not-too-rapid pace so that I didn't have much trouble keeping up.

At first chunks of Chileno Valley Road were visible behind and below us; only one car passed while we were moving and we ducked behind one of the oaks. The grassy turf was still slick with morning dew that made the footing uncertain in the steeper places; twice I had to drop to all fours and scurry sideways like a crab onto more solid ground. The oaks grew in a thick, packed belt for the last third of the climb. We zigzagged through and around them, and as we neared the top I had glimpses of the terrain below and to the north. Then they thinned out into an open area along the crown.

Chavez veered left, to a spot where a cluster of granite outcroppings rose out of the grassy earth. When I came up to him, panting and wheezing a little from the exertion, he asked if I was okay.

"Yeah. Just need a minute to rest. Getting old, slowing down."

"Not so slow," Chavez said. "When I'm your age I'll be lucky if I can make a climb like this."

"When you're my age, I hope I'm still aboveground."

He grinned, then shifted position and pointed. "There they are."

The view from next to the rocks was unobstructed and I could see all three farm buildings below. Four, if you counted what appeared to be a small well house near a gaunt, leaning windmill. The three main structures were set in a sheltered semicircle close to the backside of the larger hill—house, barn, a dilapidated outbuilding that had once been a stable, judging from the remains of a pole-fenced section along one side. A line of willows and shrubs ran at an angle behind the house and barn, indicating the presence of a creek.

When I had my wind back I uncased the Zeiss glasses, leaned against the outcropping for support, and fiddled with the lenses until the tableau down there came into sharp focus. The buildings were all at least half a century old and appeared to be suffering from neglect and slow decay. Long abandoned and forgotten. Nobody had lived there or worked the surrounding acreage in decades.

The first thing I scanned for was some sign of current occupancy. Nobody in sight anywhere. No sign of the Ford Explorer. And no barking or any other sounds drifted up on the still morning air.

"Anything?" Chavez asked.

"Doesn't seem to be."

I focused on the farmhouse. From its outward appearance, nobody had been there in years. Weathered gray boards with here and there strips and patches of old white paint like flaking skin. One corner of the roofline over the sagging remains of a porch bowed inward and was near collapse. Spiderwebbed hole in one of the front windows, the glass completely broken out of another. The front door intact and shut. A tangled climbing vine of some kind covered most of the visible side wall. On the other side was what had probably been a vegetable garden; most of the chicken-wire fencing that had enclosed it lay trampled down and rusting in the grass.

I shifted my line of sight. The rutted track petered out in what had once been a front yard: a mixture of bare graveled earth, nests of weeds and thistles, a discard scatter of boards and shingles and broken pieces of furniture. The well house and windmill stood at an angle between the house and barn, near where the creek and its fringe of trees bent away to the north; the windmill had two missing blades and part of its frame was damaged, one broken timber jutting out at right angles like the arm of a gibbet. It was difficult to tell for sure from this distance, but there might have been an irregular path of sorts angling away from the barn toward the creek; some of the weeds in that direction had a trampled look.

The barn next. Big, tumbledown, boards missing, the double doors drawn shut. But the structure itself wasn't what held my attention, led me to try sharpening the focus. Parallel ruts showed in the grassy earth fronting the doors. Tire marks stood out in the softened earth—fairly deep and fresh looking, made by a heavy vehicle such as a Ford Explorer. I followed them backward to where they thinned out and merged with the ruts in the track.

"I was wrong," I said as I lowered the glasses. "Somebody's been here recently. Have a look at the front of the barn."

Chavez took the binoculars, made his study. "Yeah, I see what you mean. Been and gone, you think?"

"Looks that way. Can't be sure from up here."

"Wait and see if anything happens?"

"That's the passive option. I'd just as soon go on down and find out one way or the other."

"Works for me."

I made one more scan of the buildings, the creek, the meadowland beyond. Everything still and empty looking in the pale morning light. Then I recased the glasses, shoved off the outcropping.

"Okay," I said. "Let's get it done."

24

JAKE RUNYON

Before he was allowed to talk to Bryn Saturday morning he had to endure more than an hour of the usual necessary legal and procedural bullshit.

First there was a consultation with Thomas Dragovich. Runyon had called him after delivering Bobby to his father and enduring another round of verbal abuse from Darby, despite the boy corroborating where he'd been and how he'd been found, and had brought the attorney fully up to date, including his suspicions as to Bryn's motives and his conviction that Bobby was innocent. But Dragovich was a careful man; he wanted to go over the questions Runyon intended to ask Bryn, to make sure they were acceptable and her rights would be protected.

Then there was a conference with Dragovich, Inspector Crabtree, and an assistant district attorney named Magda Halim. On Dragovich's advice, Runyon told them exactly what he believed and why. Neither Halim nor Crabtree seemed surprised; Crabtree admitted that he and his partner had guessed it might be the boy Bryn was protecting and had passed along their suspicion to the DA's office. Halim asked several pertinent questions—testing his honesty, Runyon thought. She was a no-nonsense ADA, probably a hard-liner in most cases; but Dragovich had told him she was also the mother of two young children and therefore might be sympathetic to Bryn's protective stance. He hoped Dragovich was right.

They sent Runyon out of the room so the three of them could talk things over. When they called him back, Halim told him he could interview Bryn, with herself, Crabtree, and Dragovich present, but that if in any way he attempted to lead or direct her, the interview would be terminated immediately. When he agreed, Crabtree called to have Bryn brought down to one of the interrogation rooms.

Dragovich took Runyon aside for another quick conference, to tell him that if Bryn recanted and cooperated fully he was pretty sure Halim and the police would be willing to release her without any further charges. So it was all up to Runyon. Handle the interview right, get her to open up, and she'd be free again.

The interrogation room wasn't one of those with the two-way glass. Nor was there any video equipment; evidently Crabtree and Halim had decided taping the interview wasn't necessary. Just four bare walls, a table with two facing straight-backed metal chairs, two other chairs set at the table ends. Familiar territory to Runyon. He'd been in carbon copies of interrogation rooms like this any number of times during his years on the Seattle PD.

A matron brought Bryn in a minute or so after the rest of them trooped in. He felt some of his tension ease when he saw that they'd let her wear her scarf; if they hadn't, her self-consciousness would've made the interview more diffi-cult. The exposed side of her face was very pale; otherwise she seemed composed in a drawn-up, girded way—a woman preparing for another ordeal. They hadn't told her Runyon would be there; her composure slipped a little when she saw him.

The matron escorted Bryn to one of the chairs at the table. Runyon took the one facing her. Dragovich pulled a third chair around on Runyon's side, but away from the table. Halim stood at the opposite end and Crabtree leaned against a wall, both of them in position to watch both Bryn and Runyon as they spoke to each other.

He said, "You holding up okay?"

"Yes. Jake, what are you—"

"I saw Bobby last night."

She blinked, leaned forward. "You did? Where?"

"Your house. I found him there."

". . . I don't understand. What was he doing in my house?"

"Hiding in the crawlspace."

"The— Oh my God."

"He ran away—took a couple of buses from the Marina. His father went there looking for him and he hid because he didn't want to go back."

"Buses? By himself? *Why?*"

"He wanted to see you. Be with you."

Choked her up. Her mouth and throat worked in little spasmodic movements; a tear wiggled down along her cheek. She started to reach a hand out across the table, a reflexive gesture that she checked in mid-motion. The hand lifted, swiped at the wetness on her cheek, then dropped back into her lap.

"Is he all right?"

"Yes. We had a long talk. Then I took him back to his father."

"Long talk about what?" She was suddenly on her guard. "What did he say?"

"The same things he said to you on Thursday."

"I . . . don't know what you mean."

"He didn't do it, Bryn. You don't have to keep lying to protect him."

"Is that what you think I'm doing?"

"It's what everybody in this room *knows* you've been doing."

"No. You're trying to trick me. . . ."

"I'd never do that to you. You know me better than that."

"I don't know anything anymore."

"The fingerprints on the knife aren't Bobby's, any more than they're yours or mine. If necessary, Mr. Dragovich will get a court order to have the boy's fingerprints taken to prove it." That was one of the legal options he and the attorney had discussed earlier.

Bryn's gaze shifted to Dragovich, to Halim, then back to fix on Runyon. Reading his eyes, trying to crawl in behind them to read his mind.

"Somebody else was in the flat that afternoon," he said. "In the kitchen with Francine. Bobby heard them talking, scuffling. Heard Francine scream."

". . . Who?"

"We don't know yet."

The good half of Bryn's mouth twisted. She reached up to touch the scarf with her bandaged finger, lowered her hand again. "Man? Woman?"

"Bobby isn't sure. Do you have any idea who it was?"

"No. No."

"He heard the door slam just after it happened. Not long before you got there. You must have just missed seeing whoever it was."

Silence.

"Did Bobby open the door for you, let you in?"

"No. I rang the bell, but . . . no."

"Was the door closed?"

"Yes, but not locked. It should have been."

"When you went in, where was Bobby?"

"He . . . In his room."

"Bloody. Blood all over his face and shirt."

"Oh, God, yes."

"Did he tell you Francine was dead?"

"Yes."

"And when you looked in the kitchen, you could tell Francine hadn't been dead very long. And Bobby was there alone."

"Yes. Alone. He was . . ."

"What was he?"

"In shock. Not very coherent."

"And you knew he hated Francine for hurting him."

"I hated her just as much. More."

"But you didn't kill her, either."

Silence.

Runyon said, "Bobby in shock with blood all over him, nobody else in the flat, her abuse, his hate. All of that together is why you didn't believe him, why you thought he stabbed her. Why you decided to take the blame."

Wavering uncertainty now. The good side of her mouth worked, but no words came out.

"Isn't it, Bryn?"

". . . Yes." In a barely audible whisper.

The others in the room stirred. Runyon reached a hand across the table, and after a moment Bryn lifted one of hers to touch his. He let himself relax then; he'd done his part.

Halim said, "You admit you lied to the police, Mrs. Darby?"

"Yes. I lied."

"To protect your son. Is that the only reason?"

"Yes."

"Are you willing to tell the truth now, cooperate freely?"

"Yes."

"Did you have anything to do with the death of Francine Whalen?"

"No, I did not."

"Do you have any knowledge of the homicide that you haven't revealed?"

"No."

Crabtree asked, "Did you touch the dead woman, disturb the crime scene in any way?"

"No."

Halim again. "Did you advise your son to lie to the police?"

"No. I told him not to talk about what happened, for his own good—that I would make everything all right. That's all."

There were several more questions, hammering at points in Bryn's original statement. She handled herself well, as innocent people usually do when they've been relieved of a heavy burden. When the ADA, Crabtree, and Dragovich had all the answers they wanted, they exited in a bunch for another conference, leaving Runyon and Bryn alone.

She had a fleeting smile for him then, after which she sat almost primly, her hands clasped together on the table. The pose struck him as a contradictory mix of young girl and older woman, of remorse and determination, sadness and hope. He felt the same protective urge he'd felt toward Bobby the night before, but he didn't give in to it this time, either. He sat without moving, letting his gaze tell her what he was feeling. This wasn't the time or the place for anything more.

In a small voice she said, "What happens now?"

"That's what they're out there deciding."

"I told the truth this time."

"I know you did. They know it, too. There's a pretty good chance they'll let you go."

"Jake . . . Bobby's really all right? I mean, not just physically?"

"He will be. Not withdrawn anymore."

"He won't run away again?"

"No. He promised me he wouldn't."

"When can I—" She broke off, started over. "Robert will try to keep me from seeing him."

"Once you're out of here, he has no legal grounds for denying you access. If he tries, we'll ask Dragovich to step in."

She nodded, showed Runyon another, not-so-fleeting smile. There was nothing more for either of them to say, not now, not here. They sat in an easy silence for several minutes, until Dragovich and Halim came back into the room.

It was the ADA who delivered the verdict: Bryn was no longer under arrest pending the outcome of the police investigation.

. . .

It took nearly two hours for the release process to be completed. Runyon waited it out by knocking around the Hall of Justice, then taking a fast walk up and down Bryant Street. Restless again, and he wasn't sure why. Something nagging at him, an irritant like a splinter he couldn't quite get hold of.

Bryn was out of there and they were in his car, winding up Market Street to Twin Peaks, when he finally pried it out. He glanced over at her, sitting in that same almost prim posture with her hands folded in her lap.

"I have to ask you something about Thursday," he said.

"Jake, please, no more questions."

"This may be important. You told Inspector Crabtree you didn't disturb the crime scene in any way. Is that the truth?"

"Yes. I didn't go near the . . . her."

"Last night Bobby told me he heard a crash, something breaking in the kitchen, just before she was stabbed. But when I was in there I didn't see anything broken."

"Oh . . . it was a plate."

"A plate."

"A plate of cookies. Broken on the floor."

"Where? Near the body?"

"No, between the sink and the center island."

"And you cleaned it all up?"

"Threw everything into the garbage under the sink, yes. That's how I cut my finger, on one of the shards."

"Why did you clean up?"

"I don't know . . . I wasn't thinking clearly. I suppose because I was afraid the mess pointed to Bobby, that the police would think he'd knocked the plate off the island when he . . . when Francine was stabbed. She must have been baking Toll House cookies for Robert; they're his favorite, Bobby's, too. . . ."

There was more, but Runyon was no longer listening.

Cookies, he was thinking. A plate of chocolate-chip cookies.

25

JAKE RUNYON

He found Francine Whalen's murderer in church. Late that afternoon, after he'd dropped Bryn off at her house and then driven immediately to the East Bay.

It was an old, well-kept nondenominational church a few blocks from Gwen Whalen's apartment building. Guesswork and an obliging neighbor who knew where Gwen worshiped were what led him there.

She was the only person in the nave, her massive body squeezed into one of the forward pews near the lectern, her head bowed. Dressed in plain black, with black hat and black purse and neatly folded black coat next to her. Mourning clothes. Thorn-crowned Christ on a bronze cross looked down on her from the wall above the altar; so did the Virgin Mary and the twelve apostles from backlit stained-glass windows. Runyon's steps made faint hollow sounds as he moved down the center aisle, but she didn't seem to notice. Didn't move when he slid onto the hard, smooth bench beside her.

"Hello, Gwen."

Her heavy chins lifted at the sound of his voice. She blinked at him without recognition at first, then with slow, dull recollection. For a couple of beats her gaze held on his; then it shifted away to peer up at the crucified Christ image. Her rosebud mouth formed silent words of prayer.

"You remember me, don't you?"

She finished praying before she said, "Yes," with her eyes still canted upward. "You came to my apartment."

"And we didn't have a chance to finish our talk."

"Mr. Runyon. A detective."

"I'd like to finish now, if you don't mind."

"Oh, not here," she said. "Not in church."

"Outside, then. Would that be all right?"

"I'm not done talking to my savior, Jesus Christ."

"When you are. I'll wait outside for you."

She didn't answer him. Closed her eyes, bowed her head again.

He left her, went out into the warmish afternoon. There was a small garden alongside the church, with a wooden bench and a fountain—a quiet place. But he wouldn't have a clear view of the entrance if he waited there. There'd be at least one other way out of the church, but he didn't think she'd use it. She wasn't trying to hide and she wouldn't run away.

Fifteen minutes before she appeared. Runyon stood as she came down the steps in her rolling, hip-swinging gait. She wore the black coat and hat now; they made her seem even larger, more shapeless.

He said, "We can talk over there in the garden."

"I have to eat something. I'll be sick if I don't eat."

"Do you want to go home instead? Or to a restaurant?"

"No. I'd rather stay here, close to Jesus."

She made no objection when Runyon put a light hand on her elbow, guided her into the garden. The bench creaked and tilted when she sat on one end. Immediately she opened her voluminous purse, brought out three candy bars: Hershey milk chocolate, Butterfinger, a triangular package of Toblerone. She tore the wrapper off the Hershey bar first, balled it, returned it to the purse, and then filled her mouth with half the candy in a series of quick, avid bites. Watching this made him wince. He felt her pain, he pitied her, but that wasn't going to stop him from adding more hurt to her already-battered emotional state.

"You like chocolate, don't you, Gwen."

She murmured something that sounded like "Comfort food."

"Chocolate milk, candy bars. What else?"

"Ice cream. Double chocolate fudge."

"And chocolate-chip cookies."

No response. She was busy devouring the rest of the Hershey bar.

Runyon said, "Fresh-baked Toll House cookies. I'll bet they're another of your favorites."

"They used to be. Not anymore."

"Not since Thursday afternoon."

He watched her open the Toblerone, shove in three wedges of the chocolate, honey, and almond nougat candy. She chewed ravenously, some of the gooey mess oozing out at the corners of her mouth. As soon as she swallowed she reached into her purse again, picked out a Kleenex, and used it to wipe the residue away.

"Tell me about Thursday afternoon," he said.

It was a little time before she answered. "Taking a life is a cardinal sin. I begged Jesus to forgive me and he has; he told me so." The rest of the Toblerone vanished. "But I can't forgive myself. Thou shalt not kill. Francine was wicked, but she was my sister. Thou shalt not kill. Jesus forgave me, but I don't think he'll let me into heaven. I'm afraid my immortal soul will burn in the fires of hell." All of this in an emotionless voice blurred by the glot of candy.

"Why did you go to see Francine?"

"The fires of hell," she said again, and her features squeezed together and for a few seconds Runyon thought she might break down. But the Butterfinger saved that from happening. He repeated his question while she peeled off the wrapper.

"Why?" she said. "Because of what you told me."

"That she'd been hurting Bobby Darby."

"I kept thinking about that. I couldn't stop thinking about it. All the things she did to me, to Tracy when we were little . . . all those terrible things. I couldn't let her keep on hurting another of God's children."

"But you didn't go there to kill her."

"Oh no. No." Half the Butterfinger in one bite. Chewing, she said, "Just to talk to her, tell her she mustn't hurt that little boy anymore. Ask her to pray with me. I remembered the man's name, the man you said she was living with in sin— Robert Darby. I looked up his address and I drove over there to see her. I didn't want to, not ever again, I've always been afraid of her, but I went anyway." Another dab at her mouth with the Kleenex. "I shouldn't have. The Devil had crept inside me that day and I didn't know it."

Runyon said nothing. No need to prompt her anymore. It was as if she were back in church, confessing to her savior—a confession he thought she would be compelled to make again and again, to anyone who would listen, for the rest of her life.

"She wasn't happy to see me. She said I was disgustingly fat, a bloated pig, a walking pile of blubber. She laughed when I asked her to stop hurting the boy and pray with me, find salvation like I have in the bosom of Jesus. She called me more names, filthy names through her candy smile. My sister, my flesh and blood. Evil."

The last of the Butterfinger disappeared. Gwen Whalen did some more rummaging in her purse, came out with another Toblerone. "I can't stop eating," she said.

Runyon looked away.

"I couldn't stop that day, either. The awful things Francine was saying to me, I wanted to put my hands over my ears, I wanted to run away, but all I did was reach for one of the cookies she'd been baking. Warm cookies on a plate, I could smell them, why should she care if I took one? But she did. She said, 'Don't touch those cookies, you fat cow' and slapped my hand. She hit the plate too and it fell and broke on the floor, but she said it was my fault. She called me a cow again, an effing cow, and slapped my face, hard."

Fat cow, effing cow. The "weird stuff about cows" Bobby had heard.

"Then she punched me in the stomach with her fist like she did when we were growing up. It hurt, it *hurt,* and Satan reared up and seized control and put the knife in my hand and I . . . She screamed and I slew her, I slew my sister. Thou shalt not kill. Her blood was on my hand, I couldn't stand to see it, I hid it inside a dish towel. Then I ran away and drove home, I don't know how but I did, and begged Jesus to cast out the Devil. He did, he forgave me, but I kept seeing Francine's face, her blood like the blood of Christ. I prayed and prayed, but they wouldn't go away. Candy smile, chocolate smile. I'm so hungry. . . ."

The second Toblerone went in two gulping bites. She pawed frantically inside the purse once more, came up with a handful of Hershey's Kisses. That was as much as Runyon could stand; he'd heard enough, seen enough, added enough to her suffering. Crabtree, Farley, Halim, somebody else, anybody else, could take over and be the next to listen to Gwen Whalen's confession.

He left her sitting there with her eyes squeezed shut again, her chocolate-smeared mouth moving silently, her fingers unwrapping more of the Hershey's Kisses—still trying to pray away, eat away, her guilt.

26

The climb down the hill was a lot easier than the ascent had been; I wasn't winded when Chavez and I reached flat ground. Still, the muscles in my legs and thighs were tight and quivery as we hurried along the rutted track. Kerry was right: I needed to get more exercise. She was always after me to go for long walks, join a gym, take up jogging again. No way on the jogging; I'd tried that a few years back and gave it up quick, mainly because I felt like an attention-drawing idiot pounding along public streets in my sweat suit. I'd feel the same way in a gym, huffing and puffing on treadmills and the other machines they have in those places. The long walks, though, were a good idea, and I'd been promising myself I would start taking them on a regular basis. Now maybe I had the impetus to follow through.

The sky was mostly clear now, the day warming up. I could feel sweat dripping under my arms, down the back of my neck into my shirt collar, as we moved ahead. The road ruts were deep and the earth between them and on either side rumpled and broken in places, so that you had to watch where you put your feet. The last thing either of us needed now was to sprain an ankle.

Once we were through the narrow passage between the hill folds, we angled ahead to where the track made its long loop to the north and stopped there. The buildings were visible from that point, with very little ground cover between. I unsheathed the Zeiss glasses for another sweeping scan. Still a frozen tableau, no sign of life anywhere. But when I had the binoculars cased again, I put my hand back on the butt of the .38 in my pocket. Never take anything for granted when you're in unfamiliar territory.

Moving again, Chavez letting me have the lead now. The hush seemed deeper here behind the hill; even the birds had quit cawing and chirping. We put a little distance between us as we came into the cluttered yard, walking on either side of the track. The ground was softer here, the ruts deeper and showing the tire indentations we'd seen from the hilltop. Fresh, all right.

The track petered out in gravel and clumps of grass, but the tire marks made a new trail straight to the barn. Check there first. The weather-beaten structure looked as if a stiff wind would knock it down into rubble: listing a little off-center, the roof caving in the middle, the entrance doors hanging crooked. When I got in close enough I saw a rusted hasp on one door half, with a padlock hanging from it by the open staple. There was a narrow gap between the two unlocked halves.

Chavez and I both drew our weapons. Then I wrapped fingers around the edge of one door, dragged it open. Its bottom scraped along the ground, making a sharp noise. I pulled harder, backing to the left, Chavez moving to my right at the same time so that neither of us was standing in front of the open doorway.

Nothing happened.

All I could see in there was gloom broken by skinny shafts of daylight slanting in through gaps in the roof and walls. We eased in, again fanned one to either side. Commingled smells of decaying wood, damp earth, mold, dust, excrement that was probably rodent generated. Something made a faint scurrying sound in the darkness. Yeah—rodents. My nostrils puckered; I started breathing through my mouth.

At first, as my eyes adjusted, I thought the cavernous interior was empty. But after a few steps I could make out irregular piles and stacks along one side, some of which appeared to be covered with the kind of plastic sheets painters use for drop cloths. I went that way, pocketing the Colt so I could fish out my keys and the pencil flash attached to the ring. Chavez came up beside me as I clicked on the light and ran the beam over what was stored there.

Cardboard moving boxes, different sizes, at least a couple of dozen. Chavez lifted one of the sheets to reveal an ornate secretary desk, a slat-backed, hand-carved rocking chair, an antique drop-leaf table, a quartet of Tiffany lamps. Under another tarp was a 48-inch flat-screen television.

"All the stuff they moved out of the house," Chavez said. "Too much to fit in that one load yesterday—three or four trips."

"Over the past couple of days, yeah."

"You think that's where they went this morning, back for another load?"

"Not after they spotted you on their tail yesterday. Too much risk."

"Well, they wouldn't leave all this here indefinitely. Too much chance of it being ruined by rats, mice, the weather."

"Right. They're planning to come back."

"But how soon?"

"When they get themselves a new set of wheels, maybe. Or a better place to hole up."

I switched off the flash and we went out into daylight. "Might be something inside the farmhouse," I said then, "if that's where they spent the night. Better have a quick look."

"I'll check around out here."

I crossed to the house, sidestepping the scattered refuse. The porch roof was held up by sagging supports, one of them cracked and bent near the roofline; the floor had a spongy feel underfoot—termite ridden and riddled with dry rot. There was no lock on the closed door. I pushed it open and went inside, testing the floorboards as I advanced.

The interior wasn't much more than an empty shell divided into six small rooms, littered here and there with the remnants of long-ago living: a broken-legged table, a cracked lamp thrust on its side into a corner, a freestanding kitchen cabinet with one door missing and the other hanging askew from its hinges. The floors were carpeted with layers of dirt, dust, broken glass fragments, half-petrified rodent droppings, all of it long undisturbed except by small four-legged creatures and now me. Nobody else had been in there in a long time. If McManus and Carson had spent the night on the property, it had been forted up inside the Ford Explorer and the barn.

I didn't linger; the dust and the mustiness of decay drove me back out into the fresh air. I was coming down off the porch, taking deep breaths to clear my lungs, when I heard Chavez shout my name.

"Bill! Over here—quick!"

He was standing near the well house, almost in the shadow of the skeletal frame of the windmill. I cut over that way, taking a zigzag route because of all the crap in the farmyard. A light, warmish breeze had kicked up, coaxing the remaining sails in the windmill into a slight, creaking turn. It wasn't until I heard the creaking that I smelled the ugly sour-sweet odor the breeze was carrying—very faint at first, then stronger as I closed in on Chavez. The hackles on the back of my neck lifted. There is no mistaking that smell and what it means.

"Inside the well house," Chavez said. He crossed himself, not once but twice. "Maybe you don't want to look."

I didn't, but I looked anyway. Had to.

He'd left the door shut. When I dragged it open, the rotting meat stink came pouring out at me. My gorge rose; I kept swallowing to hold it down while I dragged out my handkerchief and slapped it over my mouth and nose, peering ahead into the gloom. The stench was coming from within a six-foot-high circular wooden cistern. I had to force myself to go over there, stretch up, and look down into it.

Sweet Jesus.

The cistern was dry, its floor littered with bundles . . . what had once been human-sized bundles wrapped mummy-like in layers of plastic sheeting and bound with duct tape. The largest and newest of them was still mostly wrapped, but some of the plastic had already been torn away by rats. The rats had been at what was inside, too. One end gaped open and there was just enough left of the head and face revealed there to be recognizable.

Now I knew for sure what had happened to David Virden.

There was not much left of the other bundles. Remnants

of sheets long ago torn into shreds and carried away to nests; jumbles of gnawed, fleshless bones, some bleached white and some with fragments of gristle still clinging to them. There was no telling how many bodies there'd been.

McManus and Carson's victims—the ones they'd murdered since getting their hands on this property more than three years ago.

Dumping ground. Charnel house.

I got the hell out of there, still swallowing, trying not to puke into my handkerchief, and jammed the door shut tight. Chavez had backed off by several yards to escape the worst of the stink. The sick expression he wore probably mirrored mine.

He said, "The client, Virden?"

"Yeah. In there since Tuesday."

"Must be four or five others."

Rose O'Day and Gregory Pappas among them. "Yeah."

"Those women . . . Ah, *Dios*." Chavez shook his head, made the sign of the cross again. *"Monstruos."*

Monsters. Tamara's term for them, too. I was glad she wasn't here to find out firsthand just how right she'd been.

The wind was still causing the rusty windmill blades to creak; the sound had a chilling quality now, a scrape on my nerves. By tacit consent Chavez and I moved still farther away from the well house, at an angle between the farmhouse and the creek. The stench wasn't so bad there, upwind. I could breathe without the handkerchief and without wanting to gag.

My cell phone had some sort of glitch in it, didn't always pick up a signal even in the city. But it worked all right out here. I put in a 911 call to the Marin County sheriff's department, identified myself, gave the dispatcher a brief account of the situation and the address. Yes, I said, we'd be waiting when officers arrived.

But we weren't going to do our waiting back here with that stink in the air and that damned creaking. Out on the road, by the gate. That was fine with Chavez; he had no more desire to hang around this godforsaken place than I did.

We started back across the littered farmyard. But our timing was off, just a few minutes off.

We hadn't gone more than twenty yards when I heard the rumbling and rattling on the far side of the hill, low and distant, then rising. Oncoming vehicle jouncing over that uneven track. No, more than one—two distinct engine sounds, one louder than the other, moving in tandem toward the notch between the hillsides. Not county sheriff's cruisers; there hadn't been enough time.

Chavez caught hold of my sleeve.

"It's them," he said. "Coming back."

27

You don't have much time to make a decision in a situation like this. Flash through your options, pick one, take
action. Four choices here. Stay where we were in the open,
guns drawn—stand and deliver. Run for the house. Run
for the barn. Run for the shelter of the trees along the creek
behind us. We were about equidistant from each of those
last three.

The engine sounds were louder now, faintly hollow—the
vehicles grinding into the declivity. Not much more than a
minute before the lead driver would have a clear view of the
farmyard.

I said, "The barn!" and broke into a run.

Chavez didn't hesitate; he was right there beside me. There
were fewer ground obstructions in that direction, letting us
run in more or less a straight line. But clusters of weeds grew
along there, one of them a tall thistle plant that I didn't see
in time to avoid because I'd cast a quick sideways glance at
the track. I plowed through the thistle, trampling it, and its
sharp little spines snagged at my pant leg, pitched me into an
off-stride stagger. I might've gone down if Chavez hadn't

been close enough to grab hold of my arm, keep me upright and steadied.

Thirty yards to the barn, twenty, ten. He put on a burst, reached the doors a couple of steps ahead, yanked one half-open a foot or so as I pounded up. The nose of some kind of car was just poking into view. He nudged me through the opening, crowded in behind me. When he pulled the door shut behind us, it muted the approaching vehicle sounds to a low rumble.

There were chinks and gaps in the door halves that made for eyeholes. I found one, Chavez another. Both vehicles were in sight now, jouncing along the track. Neither one was the Ford Explorer. The lead car was a gray four-door Nissan compact, dwarfed by the medium-sized U-Haul truck immediately behind. Those women were no dummies. They'd sold or traded or dumped the SUV, bought or rented the compact, and then rented the U-Haul, and they'd no doubt done the buying and renting using one or the other's real name.

Both of us drew our weapons. I sucked in a couple of deep breaths, trying to slow my pulse rate, as the car and truck rattled into the yard. Sun glare on the Nissan's windshield prevented me from seeing who was driving until it turned to the right off the track. Carson. With the yellow-eyed Rottweiler, Thor, beside her. The driver's door stayed shut while the U-Haul rolled past toward the barn.

McManus was as reckless with the cumbersome truck as she'd been with the SUV in rush-hour traffic; twenty yards from the barn she made a sharp, tilting half turn in the opposite direction, braked hard, and then slammed into reverse with a gnashing of gears. The rear tires spun, digging up clods of turf, as she backed and began maneuvering.

They hadn't spotted us on the run or they'd be reacting differently out there. McManus kept backing until the rear end of the U-Haul was within a dozen feet of the doors. While she was doing that, Carson got out of the compact and the Rottweiler bounded out after her.

Chavez said in an undertone, "Coming in here. Be easier to take them if they walk in together."

"As long as they leave the dog outside."

"What if they don't?"

I waggled the .38. "What do you think?"

The barn had been the right choice. We were in perfect position to surprise McManus and Carson, take out Thor if necessary, and hold the women until the county law arrived. Good plan—except for one thing we hadn't figured on.

That damn dog and his heightened senses.

Through the eyehole I saw the animal stop moving once he was free of the car, stand with muzzle up and the big body starting to quiver. Then he was barking, loud. And then he lunged into a streak-run straight for the barn doors.

He didn't slow down when he got there. Left his feet in a sideways jump and rammed his body into one door half hard enough to splinter a couple of the rotting boards. Turned and jumped up again, nose on this time, barking and snarling and scrabbling at the wood with his nails.

"Knows we're in here," Chavez said between his teeth.

"But the women don't. Maybe they'll think he's after an animal that got in."

McManus was out of the U-Haul now, coming around to where Carson stood, both of them watching the dog's frantic scratchings at the barn door and not trying to call him off. Wary, but not alarmed yet. Neither of them looked to be armed. If they owned guns, and they probably did, the weapons would be stored in here with the other stuff. They'd have had no reason to take the guns along this morning.

I thought we might have a standoff that would last long enough for the law to show—the two women and the Rottweiler out there, us in here, nobody doing anything but standing fast. Wrong on that score, too. Because I didn't take the yellow-eyed beast's instincts into account.

He quit scrabbling at the door. Quit barking and snarling, too. I heard him moving and then I didn't hear him at all. Didn't see him anymore. I shifted position to another peephole, still didn't see him.

"Alex. You spot where the dog went?"

"No."

Not back to McManus and Carson. They were still standing together, talking to each other but looking at the barn.

Seconds ticked away, nobody moving. The silence seemed heavy, strained. Where the hell was the Rottweiler?

Pretty soon we found out.

The warning sounds came from somewhere at the side wall behind Chavez, where the half-collapsed remains of cattle stalls showed as shadow shapes in the murky light. Bumping, scratching, slithering. A deep-throated snarl. Faint blurred movement. The goddamn dog had sniffed around out there and hunted up a gap in the decaying wallboards large enough to squeeze through.

I hissed a warning to Chavez—too late. Thor was already inside and launched in a black blur. Chavez turned, bringing his revolver up, but he had no time to set himself and fire before the hurtling, snarling shape hit him straight on.

The force of impact drove him backward into the door,

wrenched a cry of pain out of him, and knocked the gun out of his hand. I heard it clatter off the boards, hit the ground. He got his left arm up in time to keep the bared fangs from tearing into his throat, but the powerful jaws locked around his forearm and the dog began to shake it the way a terrier shakes a rat.

Chavez tried to throw the animal off, but the heaving weight had him pinned. I was there by then and I kicked at Thor's ribs, his haunches; a third kick caught him square in the ass. But none of the blows did anything except bring out more growls and cause the fangs to sink deeper into Chavez's arm, shaking it even harder. For me to try wrestling the Rottweiler loose was a fool's move. I couldn't take the chance of jamming the muzzle of the .38 in against the squirming body, either, not with the poor light and the way the two of them were locked and thrashing together; if I tried that and didn't get the angle right, the bullet was liable to go right through the dog and into Chavez.

Only one thing I could do. I spun away to the row of stacked goods, jamming the gun into its holster, and tore off one of the plastic sheets. Bunched it up accordion-fashion with my arms and hands spread wide. Chavez was still struggling to break loose, grunting but not making any other sound. The Rottweiler's growls had a kind of frenzied canine elation, as if this sort of vicious attack was what he lived for.

I got in close and threw the sheet over him, ensnaring as much of the head and muzzle as I could, then managed to wrap the rest of it around the lower body and tangle up the legs. That got him off Chavez. The jaws released their hold, the muscled body twisting wildly; he let out an enraged yowl. I couldn't hold him—too much weight, too much fury.

Sharp claws and snapping teeth were already tearing tattered holes in the plastic.

All I could do was let go and jump back, set myself, and deliver another kick that caught him somewhere in the hindquarters and sent him tumbling over backward—still entangled in the sheet, but not for long. I went for the .38 again, but the sight had snagged when I jammed the weapon into the holster. I had to muscle it out, and by then the bugger had fought loose of the plastic, those yellow eyes glowing like something out of a nightmare, the big body tensing, then springing. There wasn't enough time to get off a shot. I made a clumsy, desperate effort to dodge away, knowing I wouldn't make it, sure for one terrified second that he'd rip my throat out—

Echoing report, muzzle flash.

The dog squealed, twisted, changed direction in mid-air, then dropped straight down, thudding to the ground a few feet to my left, and flopped over onto his side with mouth open and tongue lolling out. Didn't move or make another sound. Dead before he landed. Chavez had found his revolver, and by luck or skill he'd fired a kill shot and probably saved my life.

I emptied my lungs in a heaving sigh. Chavez was on one knee on the floor; I went to help him to his feet. His left arm where the jacket sleeve had been ripped away shone black with blood.

He said, "I had to risk it," in a pain-edged voice. "Glad I didn't miss."

"No risk. You had a clear shot."

Outside, there was the sudden sound of a car engine firing up.

We reacted immediately, the adrenaline in both of us still pumping. The one door half stood partway open from the force of the dog's collision with Chavez; I shouldered through it first with the .38 still in my hand.

The gunshot had galvanized Carson and McManus. They were both in the Nissan, the car slewing ahead deeper into the yard because the U-Haul was blocking the way behind. Carson, driving, couldn't make any speed because of all the refuse littering the grass; the compact bumped over something, rocking, back wheels churning for traction.

I ran toward it at an angle, slowed to draw a bead, and blew out the left rear tire. I would have done the same to the right rear or left front, but it wasn't necessary. The Nissan tipped a little, slewed, then the front end jarred into some hidden object and the engine stalled. Carson ground the ignition but couldn't get it started again. I moved closer, and as I did the passenger door flew open and McManus came out in a lurching run. The driver's door stayed shut.

McManus did not even glance in my direction. She headed straight for the track, running like a sprinter—head down, body bent forward, elbows close to her body and pumping like pistons. I yelled, "Stop!" but the command had no effect. I veered past the Nissan, stopped to brace myself, and fired a warning shot over her head. Followed it with another shout: "Stop or you're dead!" None of that had any effect, either. She didn't falter or slow down, just kept right on racing along the track.

I let her go. Even if I wasn't a little rubber legged from the skirmish in the barn, I wouldn't have been able to catch her, and I was not about to chance a leg shot to bring her down. Besides, where was she going to run to? She might make it off the property, might be able to hitch a ride with somebody or find someplace to hide, but she wouldn't stay a fugitive for long. Not with the kind of police manhunt those rat-chewed remains in the well house would generate.

I turned back toward the Nissan. Chavez had the driver's door open and was standing off a few paces, looking in at Carson, his left arm hanging loose and dripping blood. I leaned through the open passenger door to yank the key out of the ignition—a precaution even though she was no longer making any effort to get away. She didn't seem to know I was there. Her eyes were on Chavez.

"He's dead, isn't he," I heard her say as I came around the front. "Thor."

"Oh yeah," Chavez said. "Dead as all those people you killed."

The look she gave him was one of pure steaming hate—not because she'd been caught, I thought, but because the dog had been blown away. She transferred the look to me when I came up next to Chavez, then swiveled her head and stared straight ahead. Queer, what happened then: her face went blank. Literally blank, like a mannequin's. She sat unmoving, staring at nothing or at something inside her head.

I said, "Need to tend to that wound, Alex."

"Be okay. It's not as bad as it looks."

Yeah, it was. Out here in the sunlight I could see the torn flesh, the bone-deep bite marks on his left forearm. None of the bites had severed an artery, but enough blood flowed to make a red glove of the hand and fingers.

I told him I'd be right back and ran into the barn. I had to yank open three of the storage cartons before I found the kind of clothing I was looking for—silk blouses, clean. When

I came back outside with three of the blouses, Chavez was leaning against the Nissan's rear fender, his left arm cradled in against his chest, his weapon holstered and his cell phone against his ear. Making a 911 call, telling the dispatcher what had just happened and asking for an EMT unit.

"Better sit down in the U-Haul," I said when he finished, "let me wrap up that arm."

"Carson?"

"Not going anywhere." She still sat in that same motionless, blank-faced pose, her hands resting on the steering wheel; as far as I could tell she hadn't moved an inch. Automated mannequin with all the juice drained out of her batteries.

I opened the driver's door on the U-Haul, got Chavez sitting sideways on the seat, then tore one of the blouses into strips and tied the largest into a tourniquet around his upper arm. With the second blouse I swabbed the wound as best I could, fastened it in place with the rest of the strips. Finished up by making a sling out of the third blouse, tying the sleeves around his neck. Stanch the blood flow, keep the wound clean and the arm stationary until the EMTs arrived.

He endured it all with nothing more than a couple of grimaces. Tough guy, Alex Chavez. And a good man in every sense of the term—like Jake Runyon, the kind of man you could trust and depend on.

I went around and climbed onto the seat beside him. There wasn't anything else to do now except wait for the rest of it to be over.

28

JAKE RUNYON AND BRYN DARBY

"Jake, what will happen to Gwen Whalen?"

"If the public defender she draws is any good, he'll plead diminished capacity and she'll end up in a psychiatric facility."

"I don't suppose she'll ever lead a normal life again."

"There's always a chance. But she's been emotionally unstable all her life, and killing her sister put her over the line. I doubt she'll ever come back, no matter how much therapy she gets."

"That's awful. I've never seen the woman and I feel so sorry for her."

"So do I."

"Francine did so much damage to so many people . . . I won't pretend I'm not glad she's dead."

"No need to. You're entitled."

"If only she'd showed her vicious side to Robert the way she did to Bobby and her sister. We might all have been spared."

"Too calculating and manipulative to allow that to happen before they were married. But she wouldn't've been able to control herself indefinitely. She'd've gone off on him sooner or later."

"Well, he must know by now what she was underneath that sweet facade. But will he admit it?"

"He'd be a fool not to. Overwhelming evidence now."

"Yes, but he's such a cold, inflexible son of a bitch . . . I can't believe I didn't see his true nature before I married him. But he could be so sweet and charming when it suited him. . . ."

"Camouflage, like the kind Francine wore."

"He'll try to take away what little time I have with Bobby, out of spite. I know he will."

"That's not going to happen."

"How can I stop him? I told you how he manipulated the judge at the custody hearing; he'll do the same thing again—"

"His influence in the legal community isn't as strong as you think. Dragovich knows a family law attorney with a much better rep who owes him a favor."

"I can't afford another expensive attorney. I'll have to mortgage the house, take on a lot more design work, to pay my legal bills as it is. . . ."

"We've been over that. Money's not an issue—we'll work it out."

"Jake—"

"No, listen to me. Dragovich spoke to the family law guy, Jeb Murphy, and outlined your situation to him. Murphy will stop Robert from denying you visitation. And he thinks there's a good chance he can get the original custody decision reversed."

". . . Oh, Lord, could he really do that?"

"If he's as good as Dragovich says he is. Bobby doesn't want to keep on living with his father—too many ugly memories associated with the abuse and Francine's death. He wants to live with you. He told me so, and running away, coming here the way he did, proves it. He's old enough for his wishes to carry weight with any reasonable judge."

"I can't tell you what having him with me again would mean."

"Don't try. I think I know."

"I wish he were here now; I wish I could hold him, comfort him, tell him how much I love him."

"You'll have the chance soon."

"How soon?"

"As fast as the lawyers can make it happen. Murphy will contact you tomorrow morning."

"You arranged all of this? When?"

"I had a talk with Dragovich before I came over here. He's the one doing the arranging."

"But it was your idea."

"Call it a mutual resolution."

"You're such a good man. And I'm such a fool for not trusting you, lying to you the way I did."

"Let's not get into that again. You did what you felt you had to do."

"But I caused you so much trouble. . . ."

"Trouble's my business."

"Don't joke—please. I'm serious."

"So am I. Helping people in trouble is what I do, you know that. Helping people I care about makes it twice as rewarding."

". . . Will you do one more thing for me?"

"If I can."

"Stay with me tonight."

"You don't need to show me gratitude, Bryn."

"It's not that. No, really, it's not. I don't want to be alone tonight. You're the only person besides my son who makes me feel needed and I want to be close to you. You feel the same way, don't you? At least a little?"

"More than a little."

"Then you'll stay?"

"You know I will."

"And not just while it's dark. Until morning. From now on, every night we're together—until morning."

29

The woman we knew as R. L. McManus remained a fugitive approximately six and a half hours after her flight from the Chileno Valley property. Officers from both Marin and Sonoma counties, using helicopters and search dogs, found her hiding in an outbuilding on an occupied ranch three-quarters of a mile to the north and arrested her without incident.

Her real name, we found out later, was Shirley Pulaski. She and Carson, real name Veronica Boyle, were wanted fugitives, all right. In their native state, Minnesota, for grand theft and attempted murder and in Washington State for theft and coercion. They'd been working variations on the same scam for at least six years before they disappeared into their new stolen identities in San Francisco, making a total of thirteen—targeting elderly people with money and other assets who either were alone in the world or had far-flung relatives, at first ripping them off and using threats of bodily harm to keep them quiet. Pulaski and Boyle's nonviolent MO changed when one of the Minnesota victims caught wise and refused to be intimidated. They broke the old woman's neck, probably would have killed her if a neighbor hadn't intervened. It was that incident that turned the two of them into fugitives.

They'd set up another room-rental scam in Spokane, operating under aliases. A spooked victim had blown that one up, too, and again they'd managed to slip away and disappear. Likely that was when they'd headed for California and hatched their plan to steal new identities and not take any more chances on being caught by disposing of their fleeced marks. The real Roxanne Lorraine McManus and the real Jane Carson may have been their first two murder victims, each chosen as much because of the resemblance factor as for the profit motive. Odds were that no one would ever know exactly what had happened to the genuine McManus and Carson. Or to the remains of the pair's elderly prey prior to Rose O'Day.

Neither Pulaski nor Boyle had confessed to any of the crimes. They weren't talking to the police, the media, apparently not even to their public defenders. A couple of homicidal sphinxes. Didn't matter, though. There was more than enough hard evidence on the Chileno Valley property and in the Dogpatch house to convict them. In one of the boxes stored in the barn the police discovered more than fifty thousand dollars in cash and active bankbooks belonging to Rose O'Day, Gregory Pappas, and one other victim. The police also found a .32-caliber Beretta that later matched the slug the coroner removed from David Virden's skull.

When the forensic people got everything sorted out, the body count in that cistern was five—two men, three women. Virden had died of a single gunshot wound to the back of the head, no doubt on his second visit to the house; the stain on the living-room floor proved to be his blood, confirming that that was where he'd been caught off-guard and shot. The other four had been fed lethal doses of prussic acid. None could be positively identified because nothing was found anywhere for their bone-marrow DNA to be matched to.

I'm not much of a believer in the death penalty, as either a method of punishment or a deterrent, but when it comes to savagely cold-blooded mass murderers the law-and-order principles by which I've lived most of my life tend to outweigh my humanitarian sensibilites. I've only dealt with truly evil individuals a few times in my life; Pulaski and Boyle were right down there with the worst. If the DA decided to try them for multiple homicide with special circumstances, nobody would get much of an argument from me. All I'd have to do was think of their elderly victims, of what I saw and smelled inside that well house, and I might even say lethal injection was letting Pulaski and Boyle off easy.

For me, the hardest part of the aftermath was telling Judith LoPresti what had happened to her fiancé. Tamara offered to do it, but she's young and not always as tactful as she might be. The task was mine, lousy and painful as it was. I'd had to do it before, under even grimmer circumstances: telling Emily of her mother's murder three and a half years ago.

Ms. LoPresti took it pretty well. Better than most—no tears, no drama. Strong woman, the type who would do her grieving in private. Her abiding faith was the foundation of her strength. It seems to me that people who are deeply religious have an edge on the rest of us, not necessarily because it makes them better human beings but because it allows them to cope with pain and suffering on a different level of perception. Life must be a whole lot simpler and easier to take when you believe without question in God and His mercy.

A couple of nights later, as Kerry and I were getting ready for bed:

"I've been thinking about your suggestion at dinner the other night," I said, "that we should buy a second home."

"And?"

"Decided it's a good idea."

"You didn't seem very enthusiastic then. What changed your mind?"

"Well, as you pointed out, we can afford it and it'll give us a push to get out of the city more often."

"Are those the only reasons?"

"No. I'm getting too old to keep dealing with dark-side crap like finding bunches of bodies and going up against killer dogs. Damn Virden case has been giving me nightmares."

"Does that mean you're thinking of retiring again?"

"Again?"

"Well, you've been back on a full-time work schedule the past year, haven't you? Unretired?"

"True enough. And it's time I got off the merry-go-round."

"Off for good?"

I hedged on that. "I've been at it too long not to want to keep a hand in as long as I can. But there's no reason I can't cut back to the original plan—one or two days a week at the agency, no more. Tamara can put Alex Chavez on full-time—he's earned it and then some—to take over the bulk of my workload."

"You really think you can stick to the plan this time?"

"Pretty sure. A second home would help, someplace far enough away from the city to remove temptation."

"Where you could go by yourself if you felt like it, not just with Emily and me."

"Well, I wasn't thinking along those lines. . . ."

"Why not? You'll have a lot more free time than either of us, at least for a while."

"What would I do stuck out in the wilderness by myself?"

"There's no reason we have to buy wilderness property," Kerry said. "And there are plenty of things you could find to do no matter what the location. Fishing and boating, for instance. You used to do both by yourself. Any reason you couldn't take them up again?"

I admitted there wasn't.

"So we'll look for a cabin or a cottage on or near a lake or river. We could even start the hunt this coming weekend, if you're really game."

Fishing, boating, quiet days and quiet nights in the country with and without the family. Genuine semiretirement. The idea was a lot more appealing now than it had been when I'd first made up my mind.

"I'm game," I said. "The sooner the better."